This book belongs to:

_____

_____

A TREASURY OF
MAGICAL
STORIES

Over 80 wonderful tales

This edition published by Parragon Books Ltd in 2016

Parragon Books Ltd
Chartist House
15–17 Trim Street
Bath BA1 1HA, UK
www.parragon.com

ISBN 978-1-4748-5721-5

Printed in China

A TREASURY OF

MAGICAL STORIES

Over 80 wonderful tales

PaRragon

Bath • New York • Cologne • Melbourne • Delhi
Hong Kong • Shenzhen • Singapore

Contents

The Little Mermaid 6

Elsie's Aeroplane 10

The Big Freeze 12

Hoppity Rabbit's Big Adventure 16

Alice's Holiday 18

Beach Penguin 19

Adventure Balloon 20

Verity's Fairy Tale 24

As Quiet As a... 26

The Best Zoo Ever! 28

The Wedding of Mrs Fox 30

Sophie's Smile 32

Pet Pal 34

Mermaid's Treasure 36

The Dinosaur Marching Band 38

The Sparkly Princess and the Pea ... 40

Ollie's Adventure 44

The Greedy Pup 46

Mother Hulda 50

How the Tortoise
    Got His Cracked Shell 52

The Frog Prince 54

The Enchanted Shell 58

Thumbelina 60

The Peacock's Complaint 64

The Goose that
    Laid the Golden Eggs 65

Saskia's Fairy Ball 66

Max and Tallulah 68

Why the Hippopotamus
    Lives in the Water 72

How the Rabbit Lost His Tail 73

The Nightingale 74

Surf Frog 78

Bedtime Adventure 80

The Penny Wise Monkey 82

The Monkeys and the Moon 83

The Gnome 84

Rebecca Rabbit's Birthday Wish 86

The Lost Shark 88

Granny's Garden 89

The Wild Swans 90

Oscar's Best Surprise 94

Crocodile Teeth 96

The Stone Soup 97

Bird Bear 98

Cleo and the Unicorn 102

The Enormous Pancake 104

Androclus and the Lion 106

Daisy and the Genie 108

Princess Elodie's Wish Hunt.........110

Little Rabbit's Big Adventure 114

The Loudest ROAR!...................116

Darcie's Treasure..........................118

Magic Museum 119

Rapunzel.....................................120

The Clever Monkey 124

The Golden Goose 126

I Want to Be TALL! 130

Small World 132

Unicorn Magic............................136

Princess Bea's Wish 138

Poorly Bunny 140

Hazel's Comforter........................142

Rainbow Farm 143

Puss in Boots 144

The Story of the Blue Jackal 148

The Princess and the Pea 150

Pinkabella and the
    Fairy Goldmother....................154

Ella's Year 158

Rosie's Surprise 159

Cinderella....................................160

Why the Sun and the Moon
    Live in the Sky 164

Pixie Pool....................................166

Show Time!.................................167

Swimming Lessons........................168

The Snow Queen 170

Alfie and Alice 174

The Fisherman and His Wife 176

Harper's Rainbows 180

Jungle Shower..............................181

Alice and the White Rabbit 182

The Fox and the Crow 186

Balloon Adventure 188

The Butterfly Ballerina 190

The Princess and the Salt.............192

The Little Mermaid

Far, far out to sea, where the water is crystal clear, lies a secret kingdom. Here a mer-king lived with his six mermaid daughters.

The youngest was a quiet girl, with a gentle heart. She dreamed of faraway adventures in the world above the sea.

"Once a mermaid is fifteen," said her grandmother, "she is allowed to swim up to the surface. Be patient, little one, your turn will come."

One by one, the little mermaid's sisters came of age, and visited the surface. They returned full of stories of all the things they had seen.

At last it was the turn of the little mermaid. She floated eagerly up towards the sea's surface.

When she finally pushed her face out through the salty swell, she saw a fine ship floating nearby. The people were throwing a party for the handsome prince on board.

The little mermaid couldn't take her eyes off the prince.

As she swam closer for a better look, a storm suddenly sprang up and tossed the ship about on the huge waves.

The little mermaid watched in horror as the prince was thrown into the churning sea. She dived down to rescue him. Holding him in her arms, the little mermaid swam to shore and gently pushed the unconscious prince onto the beach.

When she saw some people coming down the beach to help the prince, she leaped back into the waves and swam home.

From that moment on, the little mermaid could think of nothing but the prince and how she longed to be with him.

One day, when she couldn't bear it any longer, she visited the evil sea witch.

"I can give you a potion to make you human, but I will take your beautiful voice in return," cackled the witch. "If you fail to win the prince's love, you will melt into sea foam and be gone forever!"

The little mermaid loved the prince so much that she agreed.

She swam to the shore and drank the potion, then fell into a deep sleep. When she woke up she was lying in the prince's palace. She tried to speak, but her voice was lost forever, and she could only smile at her handsome rescuer.

The prince was intrigued by the silent stranger. He took her everywhere and the little mermaid had never been happier.

Then, one day, the prince told her that he was to be married, but that he loved another girl, who had once rescued him from the sea. Without her voice, the little mermaid couldn't tell the prince that she was that girl.

On the day of the prince's wedding, the prince walked with the little mermaid along the beach. Suddenly, a huge wave crashed over the prince and the little mermaid, washing them out to sea. Without thinking, the little mermaid dived beneath the churning waves and grabbed the prince, taking him back to the shore.

"You're the girl who saved me before!" he cried.

The little mermaid smiled and nodded.

"I can't marry the princess. I love you," he sighed. "Will you marry me?" And as he kissed her, something magical happened. She could feel her voice returning!

"Yes!" she cried out with joy.

The couple were married the very next day. The little mermaid's dreams had come true, but she never forgot her family, or that she had once been a mermaid.

Elsie's Aeroplane

Elsie was a pilot. Her little aeroplane was very old and quite slow, but Elsie didn't care. She loved flying it up into the bright blue sky.

One sunny day, Elsie hurried to the airfield where her little aeroplane lived. She and her friends were going to have a race in their different kinds of flying machine. One friend flew an airliner, another had a seaplane, the third had a rocket and the last one had a jet. Each of them thought that they would be the fastest.

"Your slow, old aeroplane will come last," her friends said. But Elsie felt sure that her little aeroplane could do anything.

Elsie topped up the fuel and climbed into the cockpit. The five flying machines took off together, but they didn't stay together for long. The jet zoomed ahead. The airliner climbed high into the sky, and the rocket zigzagged around as if it were playing tag. Even the seaplane was going faster than Elsie.

"Don't worry," said Elsie, patting her little aeroplane. "I believe in you."

Suddenly, Elsie saw the airliner turn around and head back to the airfield.

"I forgot to top up on fuel," said the pilot into his crackly radio.

Then the jet zoomed off in the wrong direction. Elsie tried to tell him, but he was going too fast to listen.

The rocket flew higher and higher… and ended up in space!

"Only us left now!" said the pilot of the seaplane.

But just then, the pilot saw a lake and couldn't resist practising a water landing.

With a cheer, Elsie guided her little aeroplane over the finish line and won the race.

"We did it!" she cried. "Three cheers for the oldest, best little aeroplane in the world!"

The Big Freeze

It had been snowing all day, but when evening came, the flakes finally stopped falling. The forest was covered in a crisp, white blanket, and Scarlett the fox felt excited.

"I'll go for a walk to see how the forest looks," she said.

It was cold and the snow came almost to the top of her legs. She loved the crunching sound it made, and the way that the whole world seemed quieter.

Soon, Scarlett spotted some birds swooping and twittering high above.

"Good evening," she called. "Isn't the snow wonderful?"

"Exciting! Exciting!" the birds chirruped. "Never seen anything like it before! Amazing! Incredible! Are you going there now?"

"Going where?" Scarlett asked. But the birds were too excited to listen. They whirled and dived and looped the loop, staying high above and far ahead.

Scarlett walked on and saw her friend Rhys the owl. He was sitting on a high tree branch, hooting to his family.

"Come on," he called. "Hurry up! I don't want to miss a moment." He looked down and spotted Scarlett.

"Hello, Scarlett. What a night! What fun!"

"Hello," Scarlett replied. "I'm going for a walk to enjoy the snow. Would you like to join me?"

Rhys jumped up and down on his branch.

"Snow?" he cried. "Never mind the snow... There's something far more exciting to go and see!"

Suddenly, the owl's whole family started pushing out of the hole in the tree where they lived. Rhys was hidden among a flurry of soft feathers and excited hoots. Then the owls rose into the air and flew away.

"I wonder what he meant," thought Scarlett. "Everyone is being very strange this evening!" She started to walk faster, while overhead more and more birds were flying in the same direction. Then she heard voices and noticed a family of squirrels jumping around in the snow.

"It's magical!" one of them was shouting. "Amazing! We have to go back." Snow puffed up around the squirrels as they leaped up and down. Scarlett ran towards them to ask what was happening, but they bounded away, giggling and chattering. Scarlett chased after them. She had to find out what was making everyone so happy.

As she ran, she saw more woodland creatures fluttering and scurrying along. Even the daytime animals were there. It was as if everyone who lived in the forest knew what was going on – except Scarlett.

She stopped for a moment to catch her breath.

"That's strange," she said, panting. "We're heading towards the river, but I can't hear the water babbling and splashing like normal."

She ran on, and when she came to the river, she understood. It had frozen over like a skating rink! All the animals of the forest had gathered there for a big skating party.

As the sun
went down, the
animals fluffed up their fur and
feathers. They shared their food and helped
each other onto the ice. Scarlett wasn't very good at
skating at first. Her legs kept going in opposite directions.
But Rhys hovered overhead, giving her instructions, and the
other animals stayed beside her until she was spinning and
twirling across the ice.

All too soon, it was time to leave. Most of the animals had
already gone home, but Scarlett didn't want to go. She'd had
so much fun, she never wanted it to end.

"I won't forget the Big Freeze," she thought as she watched
two ducks sliding around the rink. "I hope the snow will stay
another night, so I can do it all again." (And it did.)

Hoppity Rabbit's Big Adventure

Hoppity Rabbit lived in a beautiful meadow at the edge of the woods. He spent his days happily running and jumping and hopping through the tall grass, chasing butterflies and playing hide-and-seek with his best friend Boppity Rabbit.

On the other side of the meadow was a large stream. Hoppity loved to watch the fish darting about through the clear, flowing water, travelling on their journey towards the sea.

"I wonder what the sea is like?" Hoppity sighed, as he stared at the fish.

"Why don't we go on an adventure to find out?" said Boppity. "Look! The fish are swimming that way. If we follow the stream in the same direction, it should lead us to the sea."

Hoppity grinned. He'd never left the meadow or been on an adventure before.

"Let's pretend we're two fish racing to the sea!" Hoppity shouted, and dashed after Boppity along the grassy bank.

After a while, the grass stopped. A long, sandy beach stretched before them. The two little rabbits couldn't believe their eyes. The golden sand was covered in endless treasures of coloured shells and pebbles, curling seaweed and little scuttling crabs.

Hoppity grabbed Boppity's paw and turned to stare at the sea.

"It's even better than I imagined!" he cried, as the waves gently lapped at his feet. "Thank you, Boppity. This is the best adventure ever!"

Alice's Holiday

Alice was so excited about going on holiday! She hopped up and down by the door while Mum checked the locks and Dad looked for his flip-flops.

"Please hurry up!" cried Alice.

It took hours to drive to the airport. Then they had to check in, queue up, show their passports and wait as the luggage was loaded onto the aeroplane.

"Too much waiting!" cried Alice.

On the aeroplane, Alice talked to Mum and Dad until they fell asleep. Then she talked to herself. "I'm too excited to sleep!" she said.

When the aeroplane landed, they had to wait for their luggage, queue up, show their passports and wait for a taxi. Alice gave a big, BIG yawn.

In the hotel room, Mum and Dad unpacked and changed into their swimming costumes while Alice rested her eyes.

"Beach time!" said Mum. But Alice had fallen asleep!

Beach Penguin

Theo the penguin loved his snowy home. He loved jumping off icebergs and swimming races with his best friend Sophie. But, one night, his iceberg home floated away into warmer water and melted. When Theo woke up, he was near a beach!

"This place is amazing!" he exclaimed, waddling onto the sand.

Theo sunbathed in a stripy deckchair. He built a huge sandcastle. He hired a surfboard and rode the waves. He caught some tiny fish in the rock pools. He even had an ice cream!

Then, when his flippers were sandy and he was getting tired, he spotted a ship heading towards his home.

"Time to hitch a lift!" said Theo, diving into the warm water.

He couldn't wait to tell Sophie about his travels — and plan his next beach adventure!

Adventure Balloon

Eloise raced across the hill, panting and giggling.

"You can't catch me!" she yelled.

Her little brother Hal was behind her, running as fast as he could. Scruffy, their dog, barked and yapped as he bounded along beside Hal.

Suddenly, they saw a big basket sitting at the top of the hill. A huge hot-air balloon was attached to it, bobbing around in the breeze.

"It's beautiful!" said Eloise. "Let's go for a ride!"

"Hurrah! An adventure!" said Hal. "Come on, Scruffy. Let's go!"

Eloise hopped inside the basket, followed by Scruffy. Hal clambered in after them and then, magically, the balloon began to rise into the sky. They floated up among the fluffy white clouds. Birds fluttered around them, twittering with curiosity. The green hills and tall trees seemed small and far away. Scruffy barked and wagged his tail.

"Where shall we go?" Eloise called to the birds.

They cheeped even louder, but the children couldn't understand them. The balloon floated far over the land and, soon, they saw a rainbow-coloured tent in a green field.

"The circus!" Hal cried, clapping his hands. "I want to go to the circus!"

At once, the balloon floated down from the sky, heading towards the field.

As it got closer, clowns, jugglers and dancers came out of the tent. "Come and join our show!" they called out.

As soon as the balloon landed, Eloise, Hal and Scruffy raced inside the tent. It was lit by sparkling stars, and colourful balloons floated down to a huge crowd.

"Let the show begin!" cried a clown on stilts.

Scruffy did flips and somersaults on the back of a white horse, while Hal tiptoed across the tightrope.

Eloise stepped onto the circus swings, thinking of the birds that had flown around the balloon.

"I want to fly like the birds," she whispered.

Then she flew from swing to swing in the high roof of the tent, ever faster and higher. The crowd went wild.

Later, at the end of the show, the top of the circus tent opened like a lid. Everyone looked up. The hot-air balloon was floating above them.

"It's time to go!" Eloise told Hal and Scruffy.

They climbed into the basket and waved to the crowds and all the circus people below.

Then the balloon rose up into the clouds again. Eloise, Hal and Scruffy clung to the basket tightly as they soared with the birds, bees and butterflies.

Suddenly, the wind died down.

"Look!" said Eloise, peering over the edge of the basket. "We're back on the hill again."

Gently, the balloon bumped down onto the soft grass, and they all tumbled out. They lay on their backs, looking up at the blue sky.

"That was amazing," said Hal.

"WOOF!" said Scruffy.

"What an adventure!" said Eloise.

She laughed as the balloon seemed to give a little hop of excitement.

"See? The balloon thinks so too," she added with a giggle. "Come on, let's go home."

Verity's Fairy Tale

Verity's family lived in a castle. Verity loved living there, as her favourite books were all about handsome princes and beautiful princesses.

Verity even hoped that, one day, a prince would visit her castle and they would have an amazing adventure together, just like in her fairy-tale books. If only her prince would hurry up!

One day, Verity was peering out of the window in the highest tower, when she heard a rumbling noise.

"The steps!" she cried. "They're collapsing!"

The winding staircase fell away, and Verity was stuck.

"How will I get down now?" she thought.

Verity looked out of the window again, but not a single prince was galloping to her rescue on a white horse. All she could see was her little brother playing football in the garden.

"There's only one thing for it," Verity said. "I'll have to rescue myself."

Thinking quickly, Verity made a ladder out of some ivy vines that were clinging to the wall outside. Then she attached them to a hook inside the tower, and climbed down through the space where the steps used to be.

Down, down, down she went, and her ivy ladder spun and swung, but she hung on tight.

At last, Verity reached the bottom of the tower.

"I did it!" she cheered.
"I rescued myself!"
And from that day on, Verity stopped waiting to have an adventure with a handsome prince... Instead, she went ahead and had them all on her own!

As Quiet As a...

Tabitha mouse was trying to sleep. But every time she closed her eyes, she heard, "CAW! CAW!" It was very loud, and it was keeping her awake. She sat up and peeped out of her window. There were seven crows sitting in a row on a telephone wire. She opened her window and leaned out.

"Excuse me, crows," she said. "Could you be a bit quieter? I'm trying to sleep." But the crows just stared at her and said, "CAW" even more loudly.

"Oh dear," said Tabitha, wondering how she could get them to understand. She put one of her tiny fingers up to her mouth and said, "Shhh! As quiet as a whisper."

The crows hunched up their shoulders and tried their best. "CSHHHHAW! CSHHHHAW!" Tabitha put her paws over her ears. It was even louder than before! She thought again, then smiled. Tapping her head, she said, "As quiet as a thought."

The crows looked at each other and shrugged. They didn't know what she meant. They all started to caw more loudly than ever, wondering what the little mouse was saying.

"No, no," said Tabitha with a sigh.

Just then, she had an idea. She scurried outside and stood on the pavement underneath the crows. She waited for them to see her, then she raised her hands to signal for them to pay attention. When they were all watching, she rose up on her tiptoes and ran up and down in front of them. Suddenly, the crows understood. Tabitha was being 'as quiet as a mouse'!

The crows shut their beaks and didn't say another word. Tabitha went back to her room, took off her dressing gown and crept into bed. She peeped through the curtains at the crows, who had tucked their heads under their wings.

"Goodnight," said Tabitha, and she lay down and fell fast asleep.

The Best Zoo Ever!

Zoe the zookeeper had just finished doing her last rounds of the day to check on the animals. Normally at this time, the zoo would be noisy with happy squawks, growls, splashes and toots. But not tonight. Silence had replaced the usual animal chatter.

"What's wrong?" Zoe asked the big grey elephant, as she passed his enclosure on her way to the main gates. "Why is everyone so quiet?"

"We're bored," trumpeted the elephant. "Nothing exciting ever happens here."

Zoe didn't want the animals to be unhappy. What could she do to cheer them up?

That night, as she lay in bed, Zoe suddenly had a great idea. She decided to call some of her friends in the morning to see if they could help her put it into action.

All of the following week, the zoo was noisy with the sound of hammering and sawing, digging and drilling. The animals looked on curiously as Zoe and her friends rushed around, wearing hard hats and tool belts, and carrying planks of wood and plastic pipes.

At last, the project was finished. Zoe called all the animals together. They couldn't believe their eyes! There, in the middle of the zoo, was the most amazing adventure play area.

"I hope this will stop you from being bored," said Zoe. "I declare this zoo-tastic park open!"

And for the rest of that day the animals played hide-and-seek in the trees and bushes. They slithered down the slide and swung from the bars of the jungle gym.

That evening, as Zoe settled the animals back into their enclosures, she smiled at all their happy faces.

"Thank you so much, Zoe!" cried the big grey elephant. "We had so much fun today. This really is the best zoo ever!"

The Wedding of Mrs Fox

Mrs Fox was feeling very sad because her husband had died.

"Don't be so sad," said her friend, Mrs Cat. "You'll soon find someone else to marry." But Mrs Fox wasn't so sure.

"I'll never find another husband as good as Mr Fox," she sighed. "He had such a beautiful bushy tail and such a lovely pointed mouth."

The next day, Mrs Cat knocked on Mrs Fox's door.

"Here's Mr Badger to see you," she said.

And in came Mr Badger. Mrs Fox could not deny that he had lovely black and white stripes, but he did not have a beautiful bushy tail or a lovely pointed mouth. So, when he asked Mrs Fox to be his wife, she turned him down.

The following morning, Mrs Cat knocked on her friend's door again. This time, she had brought Mr Squirrel to see Mrs Fox.

Mrs Fox admired Mr Squirrel's beautiful bushy tail, but he did not have a lovely pointed mouth. So when he begged her to marry him, Mrs Fox said that she would rather not.

The following morning, Mrs Cat knocked on Mrs Fox's door yet again.

"Here's Mr Mouse to see you," she said. And in came Mr Mouse.

Mrs Fox had to admit that he did have an attractive pointed mouth, but no beautiful bushy tail. So when he popped the question, Mrs Fox was flattered, but still refused him.

A few days later, Mrs Cat knocked on Mrs Fox's door again.

"There's someone to see you," she said. And in came a handsome fox. He had a lovely pointed mouth and a beautiful bushy tail. The handsome fox visited Mrs Fox every day… and soon they fell in love.

"Mrs Fox, will you be my bride?" asked the handsome fox.

"Yes!" replied Mrs Fox. And they lived happily ever after.

Sophie's Smile

All the other fish were afraid of Sophie. "She's always frowning," they said. "Why does she look so grumpy?" But poor Sophie wasn't really cross. That was just the shape of her mouth. She couldn't seem to smile and look friendly.

One day, Sophie had an idea.

"I'll throw a party," she said. "I'll show them that they don't have to be scared of me." She spent a long time getting everything ready. She sent out her invitations on tiny shells, and decorated a cave with coral in every colour she could find. She arranged for the most famous underwater band in the sea to be there, and she lit the cave with tiny crystal jellyfish.

The guests arrived and swam shyly into the cave. They looked nervous when they said hello, and Sophie's heart sank. If only they could see that she was kind and happy! But she nodded to the band, and they began to play.

"Come and dance!" she called.

One by one, the other fish started to dance. Sophie stayed back because she didn't want to frighten anyone. But as the dancers swirled faster and faster, they saw that Sophie wasn't scary at all. She was nervous, just like them!

The whirlpool of dancing fish spun Sophie, sending her topsy-turvy. She twirled around so fast that everything about her got turned upside down… including her frown!

When the music stopped playing, and everyone stopped
dancing, the other fish gathered around Sophie. They were
all smiling now they knew that Sophie was so friendly. And
when they looked at her, they saw that something about her
had changed too. Now she was wearing a big, happy smile!

Pet Pal

Betsy felt sad and lonely. Her best friend in the world, Polly, had moved away.

"Why don't we go to the park?" suggested her mum. "Or you could read a book?" But nothing was fun without Polly.

Betsy's dad came home and gave her a hug.

"Don't look so sad," he said. "I've got a new friend for you." He opened a basket and Betsy peeped inside.

"Meeow!" A sweet little kitten peered back at her.

But Betsy looked away. She didn't want a new friend. She wanted Polly!

The kitten clambered up onto the chair beside Betsy. It patted her hand with a soft paw, but Betsy pulled her hand away. So the kitten nudged her with its little nose. Its whiskers tickled Betsy's arm, and she couldn't help smiling.

"All right," she said. "Let's play."

Betsy made necklaces with coloured beads and threads, and the kitten loved to pounce on them. Then, when Betsy painted a picture, the kitten added her own pretty paw prints to the scene

After lunch, the two played hide-and-seek in the garden. Then, just before tea time, Betsy read a book to her new friend.

Betsy didn't stop thinking about Polly, but she stopped feeling so sad. Instead, she thought about how much Polly would like the kitten.

After tea, the kitten curled up on Betsy's lap. Betsy wrote a letter to Polly. She had lots to say! She told Polly all about the little kitten and the things they had done together. It was fun to remember their adventures.

"I still miss you very much," she wrote. "But I think I will enjoy writing letters to you. And my new kitten will make sure I have plenty to tell you!"

Mermaid's Treasure

One morning, Pearl the mermaid was playing around a reef when she spotted a large sea chest among the coral. She swam closer.

"It must have fallen out of a ship," she exclaimed. "I wonder what's inside!"

But when she tried to lift the lid, she found that it was locked.

"Oh, bother," Pearl muttered. "Now I want to look inside even more!"

She tried to force the lid open with a clam shell, but it wouldn't budge. So she asked her biggest, strongest friends for help.

Shark tried to bite a hole in it. Octopus wrapped his tentacles around the chest and tried to squeeze it open. Whale tried crushing it with his weight.

"It's no use," sighed Pearl. "We'll never get it open."

"May I try?" said a squeaky voice in her ear.

Pearl turned and saw a tiny shrimp, no bigger than her fingernail. She smiled at him. How could someone so small open the chest?

"Of course you may," she said politely.

The little shrimp wriggled through the keyhole. Pearl, Shark, Octopus and Whale watched as he reached into the lock with his spindly legs. Then there was a loud click, and the chest unlocked.

The shrimp swam out, looking very pleased with himself.

"Well done!" cried Pearl.

Slowly, she lifted the lid. The chest was full of men's clothes! Pearl sat back and laughed loudly.

"Some poor sailor has lost his luggage," she chuckled. "I suppose it would be treasure to him!"

She looked at her friends and laughed again.

"Don't look so disappointed," she went on. "We may not have gold or jewels, but we've made a very clever friend."

And the little pink shrimp blushed bright red!

The Dinosaur Marching Band

One, two, three, four! Keep it up, two, three, four!
The jungle rumbles and the ground shakes.
CRASH! THUMP! What's that sound?

Oh, look! It's the dinosaur marching band, and they're coming this way! Crashing, stomping, singing and playing their loud music as they sway through the trees.

STOMP! STOMP! TOOT! TOOT! BANG! BANG!

What an impressive noise they make!

Tommy T. Rex is at the head of the line. He leads his fellow musical marchers, tooting loudly on his golden trumpet, the melody floating on the air.

Following closely behind is Daisy Diplodocus. With a steady beat on her jungle drums, she sways her long neck and stamps her large feet, keeping the rhythm for the rest of the band.

Susie Stegosaurus sings her sweet, soulful song, hitting the high notes perfectly. LA, LA, LA, LA, LA!

Then there's Terry Pterodactyl, flying above his marching friends. He whistles the melody with Tommy's crisp trumpet notes, while Arthur Ankylosaurus hammers a bass beat on the ground in time with Daisy's drums.

And, last but not least, Trixie Triceratops stomps along at the back of the line, keeping time as she counts: "One, two, three, four! Keep it up, two, three, four!" She shouts out the numbers with a noisy ROAR!

STOMP! STOMP! TOOT! TOOT! BANG! BANG!

It's the wonderful musical dinosaur marching band… and they're coming your way.

The Sparkly Princess and the Pea

Once upon a time, there lived the most sparkle-tastic princess EVER! Her name was Glitterbelle.

Glitterbelle loved anything glittery, shimmery and purple. She also loved playing with her friends and climbing trees.

But there was something that Glitterbelle definitely did not love, and that was PEAS! She thought they were squishy, gross and very… green.

"How do you know you don't like peas if you won't even try them?" asked King Alfie, one dinner time. "We love them. In fact, we owe our kingdom to peas."

"It's how your great-great-great-great-grandpapa found your great-great-great-great-grandmama," added Queen Lizzie. "Remember the famous fairy tale?"

"Yes, I know," said Glitterbelle, with a sigh. "It's the one where great-great-great-great-grandmama had to prove to everyone she was a REAL princess by feeling one tiny pea under twenty mattresses."

"That's it," grinned King Alfie. "And we've still got that very same pea. It'll be yours some day!"

Glitterbelle looked at the dried-up pea, proudly sitting in a dusty glass case. "Yuck!" she groaned.

Just then, Glitterbelle's best friends Dazzlina, the witch, and Angel, the ballerina, came round to play at the palace. Sighing, Glitterbelle told her friends how much she hated peas.

"I must be the first princess EVER not to like them!" she said. "Maybe I'm not really a princess after all."

"Well, you do like climbing trees," said Angel thoughtfully.

"And racing around on your scooter," added Dazzlina. "They're not very princessy things to do."

"I knew it!" cried Glitterbelle. "I am different to fairy-tale princesses."

"We're only teasing you," laughed Dazzlina.

"We love you whether you're a fairy-tale princess or a scruffy, tree-climbing one," added Angel with a smile.

"Thanks," replied Glitterbelle. "But I don't feel like any kind of princess right now."

After her friends had left, Glitterbelle was still feeling sad.

"What's wrong?" asked Queen Lizzie at bath time.

"I'm not a proper princess," cried Glitterbelle. "I don't act like one or look like one. I'm too ME to be a princess!"

"Oh, Glitterbelle," said Queen Lizzie, "you're a proper princess just by being you!" She hugged her daughter. "It will all seem better in the morning, I promise."

After her bath, Glitterbelle went downstairs to drink some hot cocoa. Meanwhile, Queen Lizzie had an idea. She could prove to Glitterbelle that she really was a princess!

Smiling, the queen popped something small, round and green under the mattress on Glitterbelle's bed.

That night, Glitterbelle tossed and turned – she barely slept a wink! The next morning, Glitterbelle woke up, aching all over.

As she climbed out of bed, a small green pea rolled out from under her mattress. The princess picked it up and knew at once why she hadn't been able to sleep.

The tiny pea proved that Glitterbelle was a fairy-tale princess after all, just like in the famous story.

"Mum! Dad!" Glitterbelle shouted, racing downstairs.
"Look! This LOVELY pea proves that I'm a real princess."

"We always knew you were," smiled the queen. "As well as being our special Glitterbelle princess, of course."

Glitterbelle beamed at her mum, then looked at the pea. "Maybe peas aren't so bad after all," she said.

The king and queen laughed.

"I think we should have a party to celebrate," said the king.

And all of Glitterbelle's friends and family were invited.

Later, when everyone sat down to a tasty banquet, Glitterbelle spotted a green cake… It had been made with a special ingredient – peas! Glitterbelle ate her slice, and smiled.

"This pea-green cake is delicious!" she said.

"You're a REAL fairy-tale princess now," giggled Dazzlina.

"Of the Glitterbelle kind!" added Angel.

Ollie's Adventure

One day, Ollie the dolphin was playing in the deep, bubbly ocean. His mum was nearby, but he was busy doing somersaults, twirls and loops. Then, all of a sudden, Ollie was alone. He couldn't see his mum anywhere.

"Mum!" he called. "Where are you?" The ocean suddenly seemed very big.

Soon, Ollie saw a crab scuttling along the seabed.

"Will you help me find my mum?" Ollie asked.

The crab clicked his pincers. "I'm too busy to look for dolphins," he snapped, so Ollie swam on.

After a while, Ollie came to a big underwater cave. An octopus floated out towards him.

"Have you seen my mum?" Ollie asked.

The octopus shook his head.

"Ask the jellyfish," he said. But the glowing jellyfish just shrugged, then opened and closed like an umbrella.

"Oh dear," said Ollie. "How am I ever going to find my way home?"

Then, suddenly, Ollie remembered something.

"If you ever get lost, I will wait for you next to the big shipwreck," his mum had told him.

Ollie darted after the jellyfish. "Which way is the big shipwreck?" he asked.

This time, the jellyfish knew the answer. "I'll light the way!" she said.

As they passed the cave, Ollie called out to the octopus, "We're on the way to the shipwreck!"

"I know where that is!" boomed the octopus. He used his tentacles to point the way.

Even the crab helped to lead Ollie to the big shipwreck. And there beside it was…

"Mum!" Ollie darted towards her and they rubbed noses.

"I'm so happy you remembered our meeting place," said Ollie's mum.

"Me too," said Ollie. "And now I know my way here, I will never get lost again!"

The Greedy Pup

Mr and Mrs Dog were very busy animals. They had five puppies to look after! Chocolate and Coffee had brown spots, Sunny and Daffodil had yellow spots, and Custard was yellow all over.

Custard's brothers and sisters were always being called 'good dog'. They never barked too loudly or chewed up slippers. They never jumped on the sofa or got mud on their collars.

But Custard was always up to mischief… especially when it came to food. If there were snacks to be found, then you could be sure that Custard would find them.

One morning, the Dog family were eating their breakfast together. Chocolate and Sunny had a friendly tug of war, while Daffodil and Coffee gnawed on their bones. Custard, who had already finished his bone, saw that no one was looking and drank everyone else's milk. His tummy gave a loud rumble.

"Was that thunder?" asked Mr Dog.

"Where has all the milk gone?" asked Mrs Dog.

Custard thought that this was a good time to go for a walk. He was still hungry after breakfast, and he was very good at finding a few extra titbits to keep him going until lunchtime.

First, he visited the hot dog stand at the end of the road. He rose up on his hind legs and panted. The man selling hot dogs grinned at him.

"All right, you cheeky pup," he said. "Have a hot dog!" He flipped a hot dog into a bun and smothered it in tomato sauce. Then he sent it spinning through the air, and Custard caught it and ate it up in three gulps.

But Custard was still hungry, so he ran down to the ice-cream stall. The ice-cream seller was busily mixing different flavours.

"Hello, Custard!" she exclaimed. "Will you help me taste some new flavours?"

Custard could hardly wait. He tried mint and raspberry, and caramel and banana, but his favourite was apple and cinnamon. He had three scoops, a cone and a flake.

47

Next, Custard visited his friend Patch's café. All the customers smiled when they saw him licking his lips. One shared their toast with him, another gave him some scrambled egg, while a third handed him a plate of baked beans, sausages and grilled tomatoes. Custard wolfed it all down.

Soon, Custard started to make his way home. He was beginning to feel a bit full.

The ginger cat on his street had a bowl of cat treats outside her house. She offered some to Custard. He tried one, but he didn't like it at all.

"Now I feel really full," he thought.

The dog on the corner had a bowl full of delicious-looking biscuits, but Custard didn't ask to share it. He padded by without even as much as a sniff.

Custard was almost home when he spotted a large cake sitting on the doorstep outside his house. It had yellow icing with white flowers all over it. Custard looked around, but no one seemed to own it.

"It wouldn't be fair to leave this cake here on its own," he said. "Cakes are meant to be eaten. Even if I don't want it, I know my family will!"

He carefully picked up the plate in his teeth and took it inside. His mother was waiting for him.

"Custard, you naughty pup," she started to say. Then she stopped and looked at the cake he was carrying.

"You found it!" she cried. "I couldn't remember where I'd put it... We were going to surprise you with it after breakfast!"

Custard put the plate down and saw the writing on the top. "HAPPY BIRTHDAY, CUSTARD!"

"I forgot it was my birthday!" he said. "Thanks, everyone."

But Custard was still not feeling hungry. So he let his family tuck into the cake.

Barking and cheering, his brothers and sisters bounded over. Soon the whole cake had disappeared. Then they snuggled up together and snoozed in the family basket.

Custard smiled in his sleep. He didn't mind about not eating his birthday cake… he knew a lovely bakery around the corner. He might visit it tomorrow!

Mother Hulda

There was once a woman with two daughters. Her stepdaughter was hard-working, while her own daughter was lazy. The woman preferred her birth daughter, and made her stepdaughter do all the work around the house.

One day, the woman gave her stepdaughter an enormous basket of wool.

"Take this wool and spin it all. Don't come back until it's finished," she told her stepdaughter.

So the stepdaughter sat and spun until her fingers bled. Just as she lowered a bucket into the well, ready to scoop up some water to wash her fingers, she accidentally dropped the spindle. It fell into the water at the bottom of the well with a PLOP!

The girl climbed down to find the spindle and, at the bottom of the well, she found herself in a strange land with orange trees, blue grass and a pink sky.

After a while, she reached a little house. A kind woman called Mother Hulda lived there. She gave the girl food and shelter.

In return, the girl helped Mother Hulda with all her chores.

Even though Mother Hulda was kinder than her stepmother, the girl began to feel homesick.

"I would like to return home," said the girl.

So Mother Hulda gave the girl back her spindle and, as the girl left the strange land, a shower of gold coins fell at her feet.

When the girl arrived home with the coins, her stepmother was amazed. She wanted the same thing to happen to her own lazy daughter.

"Do just as your sister did," she told the idle girl.

But the stepmother's daughter could not be bothered to sit and spin, so she stuck her hands into a thorny bush to make them bleed. Then she dropped the spindle down the well and climbed in after it.

The girl knocked on Mother Hulda's door, asking for food and shelter. After eating, she fell asleep, snoring like a pig!

"Give me back my spindle. I want to go home now," said the rude girl to Mother Hulda when she woke up.

So Mother Hulda took the girl back to the bottom of the well. But instead of gold coins, it was tar that fell at her feet.

The girl returned to her mother, who tried to scrub her shoes clean. But the tar was stuck fast, and has remained there ever since.

How the Tortoise
Got His Cracked Shell

Once upon a time, there lived a tortoise. He was very sly and the other animals didn't like him.

One day, all the birds were invited to a party in the sky. Tortoise wanted to go too, so he came up with a cunning plan. He told the birds that they would need a leader to do all the talking when they arrived at the party.

"I would make the best leader," he said, "because I am so good at talking!"

Although the birds didn't like Tortoise, they agreed that he was indeed very good at talking. Each bird gave one feather to Tortoise. He stuck them on his shell so that he could fly up to the sky with them.

Before they left, Tortoise told the birds that they would all need to choose a name, so they could introduce themselves at the party.

"My name will be 'All of You'," he said.

When they arrived at the party and the food was brought out, Tortoise asked their hostess, "Whose food is this?"

The hostess replied, "This food is for all of you."

Tortoise turned to the birds.

"This food is for me. Perhaps they will bring out your food later?" And he ate all the food.

The birds didn't get anything to eat. They were very angry, and took back all their feathers from Tortoise's shell.

Tortoise couldn't fly home without the feathers. He begged the birds to take a message to his wife. Finally, Parrot agreed.

"Tell my wife to lay out pillows so that I will have a soft landing when I jump from the sky."

However, when Parrot saw Tortoise's wife, he told her to lay out all the sharpest things she could find.

At a signal from Parrot, Tortoise jumped.

Down he fell, and then CRACK! went his hard shell!

Afterwards, Tortoise's wife took him to the doctor. The doctor was able to put Tortoise's shell back together, but it was never smooth again.

And that's why all tortoises have cracked shells.

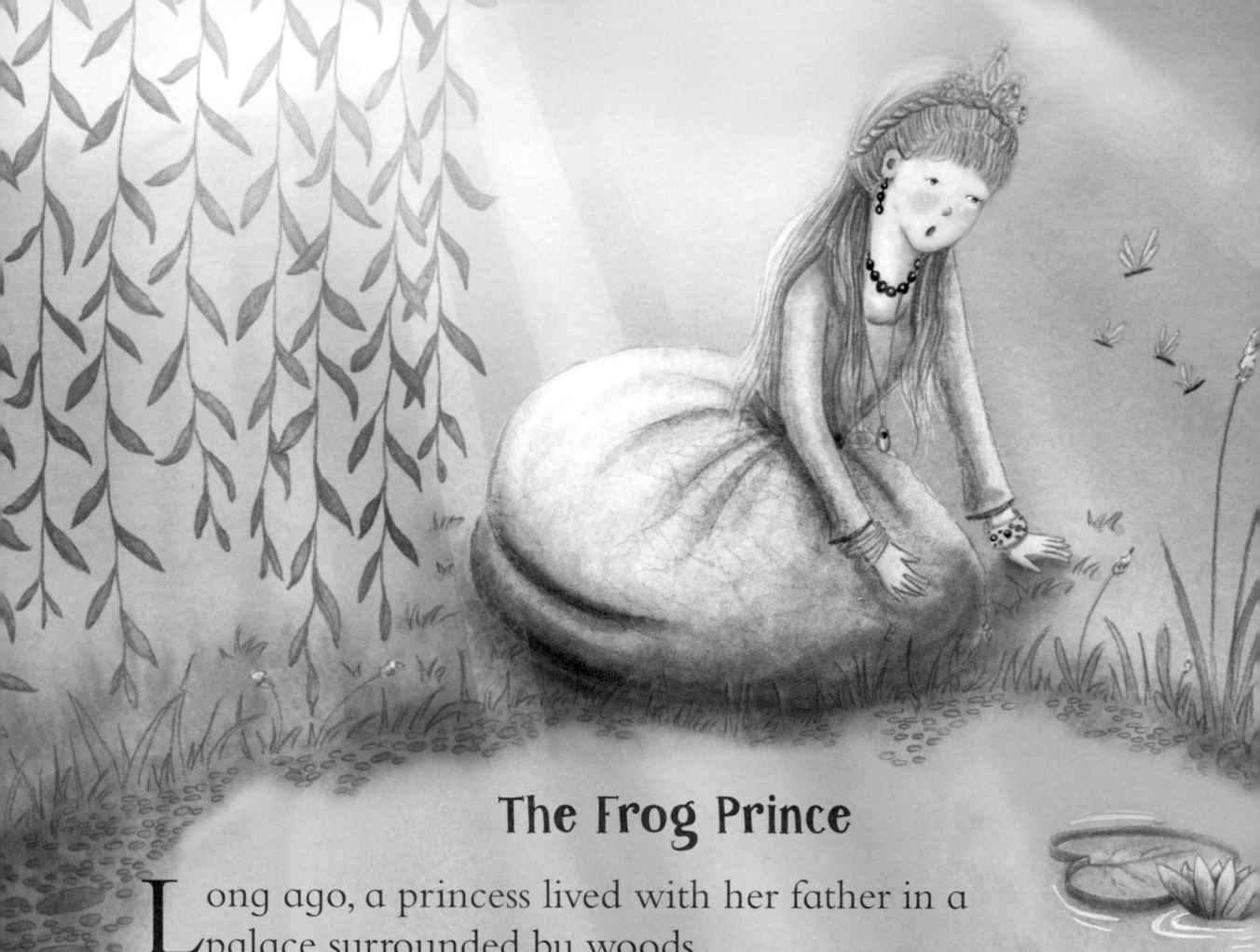

The Frog Prince

Long ago, a princess lived with her father in a palace surrounded by woods.

When it was hot outside, the princess would walk into the shade of the forest and sit by a pond. There she would play with her favourite toy, a golden ball.

One day, the ball slipped from her hand and fell to the bottom of the pond. "My beautiful golden ball," she sobbed.

An ugly, speckled frog popped his head out of the water. "Why are you crying?" he croaked.

"I've dropped my precious golden ball into the water," she cried.

"What will you give me if I get it for you?" asked the frog.

"You may have my jewels," sobbed the unhappy princess.

54

"I don't need those," said the frog. "If you promise to care for me and be my friend, let me share food from your plate and sleep on your pillow, then I will bring back your golden ball."

"I promise," said the princess, but she thought to herself, "He's only a silly old frog. I won't do any of those things."

When the frog returned with the ball, she snatched it from him and ran back to the palace.

That evening, the princess was having dinner with her father when there was a knock on the door.

When the princess opened the door, she was horrified to find the frog sitting there. She slammed the door and hurried back to the table.

"Who was that?" asked the king.

"Oh, just a frog," replied the princess.

"What does a frog want with you?" asked the puzzled king.

The princess told her father about the promise she had made.

"Princesses always keep their promises," insisted the king. "Let the frog in and make him welcome."

As soon as the frog hopped through the door he asked to be lifted up onto the princess's plate. When the frog saw the look of disgust on the princess's face, he sang:

"Princess, princess, fair and sweet, you made a special vow
To be my friend and share your food, so don't forget it now."

The king was annoyed to see his daughter acting so rudely. "This frog helped you," he said. "And now you must keep your promise to him."

For the rest of the day, the frog followed the princess everywhere she went. She hoped that he would go back to his pond when it was time for bed, but when darkness fell, the frog yawned and said, "I am tired. Take me to your room and let me sleep on your pillow."

The princess was horrified. "No, I won't!" she said rudely. "Go back to your pond and leave me alone!"

The patient frog sang:

56

"Princess, princess, fair and sweet, you made a special vow
To be my friend and share your food, so don't forget it now."

Reluctantly, the princess took the frog to her room. She couldn't bear the thought of sleeping next to him, so she put him on the floor. Then she climbed into her bed and went to sleep.

After a while, the frog jumped up onto the bed. "It's draughty on the floor. Let me sleep on your pillow," he said.

The sleepy princess felt more annoyed than ever. She picked up the frog and hurled him across the room. But when she saw him lying dazed and helpless on the floor, she was suddenly filled with pity.

"Oh, you poor darling!" she cried, and she picked him up and kissed him.

Suddenly, the frog transformed into a handsome young prince.

"Sweet princess," he cried. "I was bewitched and your tender kiss has broken the curse!"

The prince and princess soon fell in love and were married. They often walked in the shady forest together and sat by the pond, tossing the golden ball back and forth, and smiling at how they met.

The Enchanted Shell

Anna lived in a big, white house by the sea. She loved to watch the sun go down behind the waves and listen to the splashing of the surf.

One evening, she was walking along the beach when she saw a pearly pink shell lying on the sand.

"How pretty!" she said, picking up the shell. Suddenly, the shell started to sparkle. Then it rose into the air and flew into the sea, where it grew bigger and bigger, until it was the size of a small boat!

Anna climbed into the shell and it took her further and further out to sea.

The stars came out, and moonlight danced on the water. Fish in all the colours of the rainbow swirled around the shell, making it spin slowly. A purple octopus peeped over the side of the shell and smiled at Anna.

From beneath the water, music rose up. It was the most wonderful music that Anna had ever heard. Then a beautiful mermaid appeared.

"My sisters and I make music every night," said the mermaid. "The octopus will look after your boat. Come and play!"

Anna slipped into the water and the mermaid led her to a glimmering blue-green palace under the sea. Mermaids danced around Anna, their tails twinkling.

Anna stayed with the mermaids until the stars disappeared and the sun came up. It was time to leave. Anna swam to the boat and it carried her back to the beach by her home.

Walking home, Anna held tightly to the little shell. She knew that more adventures would find her whenever she visited the beach with the special shell in the moonlight!

Thumbelina

Once upon a time, there was a poor woman who lived all alone. She dreamed of having a child of her own with whom she could share her home. One day, she decided to visit a kindly witch that lived at the end of her lane to ask for help.

"Take this grain and plant it in a pot," said the witch. "Water it and care for it. The grain will do the rest."

Every morning the woman checked on her precious plant. Within a week, it had grown into a tall flower.

"I've never seen anything as beautiful," said the woman, bending down to give the bud a gentle kiss.

POP! The pink flower suddenly opened up its petals. Sitting inside it was a tiny girl, no bigger than the woman's thumb. The woman was overjoyed.

"I shall call you Thumbelina," she cried.

Thumbelina and her mother were very happy. Then, one night, while they slept, a warty toad took Thumbelina away.

"You will make the perfect wife for my son," hissed the toad, placing Thumbelina on a lily pad in the middle of a stream. Then the toad swam off to find her son.

Poor Thumbelina started to cry – she didn't want to marry a toad.

"Don't cry, little girl," said a passing fish. "I'll help you."

The kind fish nibbled through the stem of the lily pad and it floated free downstream. At last, it drifted to the riverbank, and Thumbelina jumped off.

All summer, Thumbelina lived happily among the flowers. But when winter arrived, she was cold and hungry.

A kind field mouse invited her to spend the winter in his cosy underground burrow. It was warm and snug, but Thumbelina missed the sunlight.

One day, the mouse's friend, a mole, asked Thumbelina to marry him. Thumbelina didn't want to marry the mole and live underground. But, as the mouse had been so kind to her, Thumbelina agreed to a wedding the following summer.

As the wedding day grew closer, Thumbelina became more sad. One morning, she was miserably wandering through the underground tunnels of the mouse's home, when she came across a swallow. He was almost dead with cold.

"I will help you," said Thumbelina, hugging the bird to her.

"Thank you," sighed the swallow, "you have saved my life. I will take you to a place where the sun always shines."

Tears ran down Thumbelina's cheeks. "I can't leave," she cried. "I have to marry Mole."

"I will never forget what you have done for me," said the swallow, and he left.

Summer came around again, and the day of Thumbelina's marriage to Mole. As Thumbelina stepped outside to say goodbye to the sunshine forever, the swallow swooped down.

"Quick, come with me!" he chirped. And this time Thumbelina didn't refuse.

The land of sunshine was full of beautiful flowers. As Thumbelina reached out to touch a pretty bud, its petals opened to reveal a tiny fairy prince.

All around her, little fairies appeared.

"Will you marry me?" asked the tiny prince.
"I will!" replied Thumbelina, grinning joyfully. She knew she had found the place where she truly belonged.

The Peacock's Complaint

Peacock was very unhappy about his ugly voice, and he spent most of his days complaining about it to anyone who would listen.

One day, Fox had had enough of Peacock's constant moaning.

"It is true that you cannot sing," he said, "but look how beautiful you are. Your feathers are amazing!"

Peacock looked at his feathers.

"Oh, what good is all this beauty," he groaned, "if I have such an unpleasant voice?"

Fox sighed. "Everyone has their own special gift. You have your beauty, the nightingale has his song, the owl has his eyes, and the eagle has his strength."

But Peacock continued to moan.

"Even if you had a musical voice," Fox shouted in frustration, "you would find something else to complain about!"

And the moral of this story is: Do not envy the gifts of others. Make the most of your own.

The Goose that Laid the Golden Eggs

A farmer and his wife owned a very special goose. Every day, the goose would lay a golden egg. The couple sold the eggs and, before long, they became rich.

The goose continued to lay her golden eggs and the farmer and his wife got richer and richer. But, sadly, they also became greedy. In spite of their great wealth, they were not satisfied.

One day, the farmer's wife turned to her husband and said, "Just think, if we could have all the golden eggs that are in this goose, we could be even richer, even more quickly!"

The farmer grinned at his wife.

"You're right," he cried. "We wouldn't have to wait for her to lay an egg every day."

So, the greedy couple killed the goose. Of course, she was like every other goose. She had no golden eggs inside her at all. And that was the end of the golden eggs!

And the moral of this story is: Too much greed results in nothing.

Saskia's Fairy Ball

Saskia the fairy was organising the fairy ball. But, on the morning of the ball, she lost her wand!

"How am I going to get everything ready for tonight without magic?" she cried.

Suddenly, she had an idea. She was good friends with the woodland animals, and she had been planning to invite them all. Perhaps they would help her!

First, Saskia had to find a place to hold the ball. Without her wand, she couldn't build a palace, so she chose a little clearing in the forest. Next, she visited the squirrels and rabbits, and explained her problem.

"Will you help me?" she asked. "I need food, decorations and music."

"We can make nut muffins," the squirrels squeaked.

"Carrot cupcakes!" the rabbits cried, hopping around.

Saskia flew up to the treetops to visit her magpie friends.

"You love sparkly things," she said. "Will you find decorations for the trees?"

The magpies agreed and flew off. Finally, Saskia asked the fireflies to light up the ball and the songbirds to provide the music.

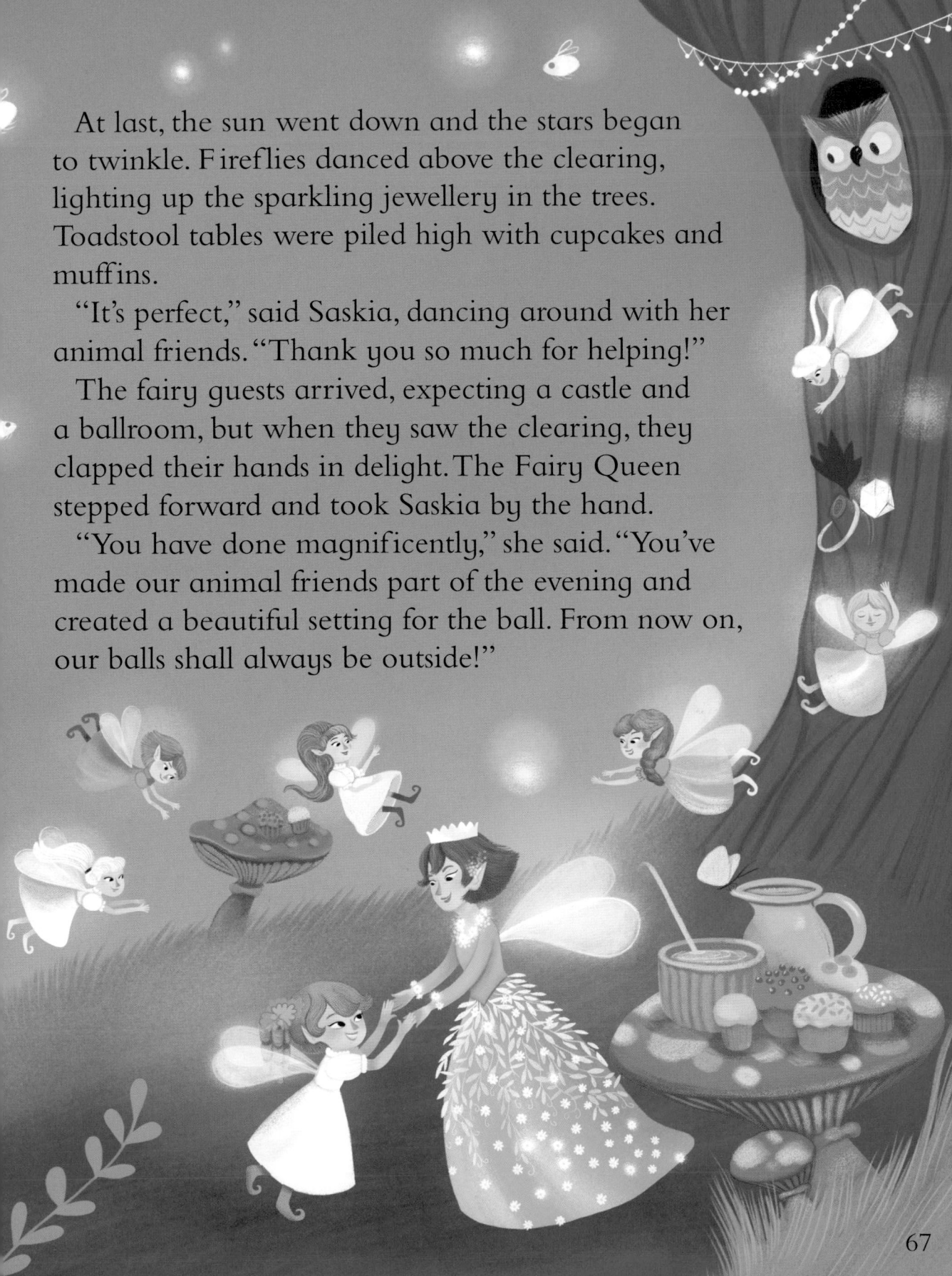

At last, the sun went down and the stars began to twinkle. Fireflies danced above the clearing, lighting up the sparkling jewellery in the trees. Toadstool tables were piled high with cupcakes and muffins.

"It's perfect," said Saskia, dancing around with her animal friends. "Thank you so much for helping!"

The fairy guests arrived, expecting a castle and a ballroom, but when they saw the clearing, they clapped their hands in delight. The Fairy Queen stepped forward and took Saskia by the hand.

"You have done magnificently," she said. "You've made our animal friends part of the evening and created a beautiful setting for the ball. From now on, our balls shall always be outside!"

Max and Tallulah

Max loved Tallulah with all his heart. But he was too shy to tell her. If only there was a way to make her notice him.

So Max decided to give Tallulah a present. He picked her favourite fruit, balanced it on a lily leaf and pushed it carefully along the river.

But just before Max reached Tallulah, the leaf started to sink! All the fruit fell into the water and floated away.

Max needed another plan.

That night, by the light of the moon, Max practised a daring dance.

When the sun began to rise, he went to find Tallulah.

Tallulah was in the forest looking for juicy leaves. Max was certain his daring dance would get her attention.

He stepped forward, tapped his hoof and leaped into the sky. Then he twirled, faster and faster!

Surely Tallulah would notice him now?

But Tallulah was so busy eating that she didn't see Max or any of his daring dance.

Max needed a new idea.

He gathered leaves and flowers and insects of every size and colour. Max was going to make the most magnificent hat Tallulah had ever seen!

Surely that would impress her?

But when Max appeared in his magnificent hat… Tallulah was so startled that she ran away!

Max had not meant to frighten Tallulah. What could he do now?

Suddenly, Max saw his reflection in the water and he had the greatest idea of all!

He was going to be…

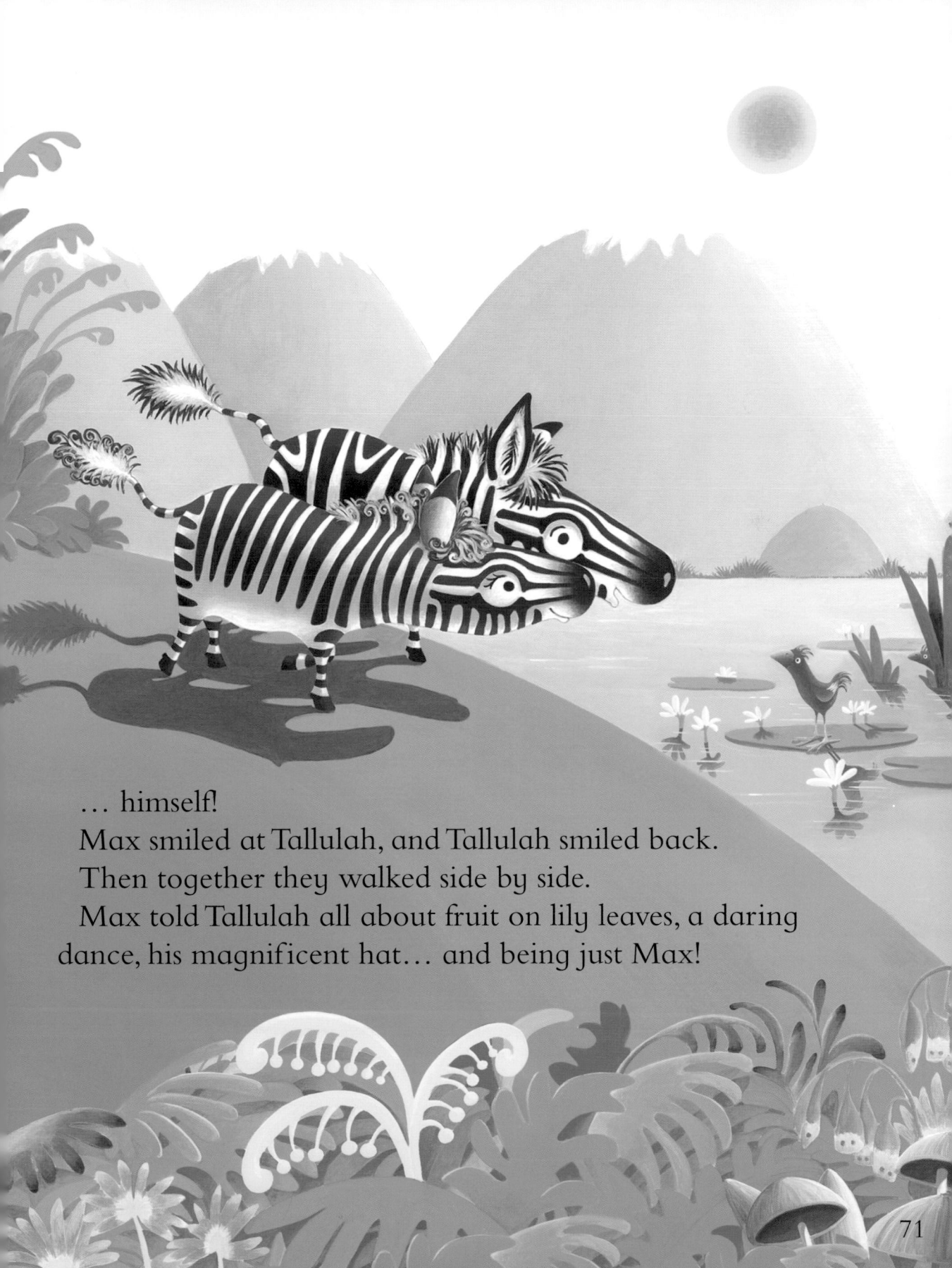

… himself!

Max smiled at Tallulah, and Tallulah smiled back.
Then together they walked side by side.

Max told Tallulah all about fruit on lily leaves, a daring
dance, his magnificent hat… and being just Max!

Why the Hippopotamus Lives in the Water

A long time ago, there was a huge hippo. Nobody except the hippo's family knew his name.

One day, the hippo asked the other animals to guess his name. But, as the hippo had suspected, no one could get it right.

"What would you do if I told you your name?" asked a little tortoise.

"I would be so ashamed that my family and I would leave the land to live in the water," replied the hippo. "We would only come out at night to feed."

Soon, after noticing that the hippo and his family washed and drank in the lake every day, the tortoise hid by a bush and waited until they were returning home.

As the hippo's wife trailed behind her family, the tortoise crept onto the path in front of her, then tucked into his shell.

"Ouch!" cried the hippo's wife, as she bumped into the tortoise's hard shell. "Isantim, my husband, I've hurt my foot!"

Later, the tortoise told the hippo his name and Isantim kept his promise. And that's why hippopotamuses live in the water.

How the Rabbit Lost His Tail

Mrs Cat was very jealous of Mr Rabbit's long tail, as she didn't have one. So Mrs Cat stole Mr Rabbit's fine tail. Then she took a needle and thread out of her basket and sewed the tail onto her own body.

"It looks so much better on me!" Mrs Cat purred happily.

"I found my tail too long, anyway," Mr Rabbit replied. "You can keep it if you give me your basket." So she did.

And Mr Rabbit hopped off into the forest with the basket.

"I've lost my tail, but I've gained a basket," he thought. "Maybe I'll find a new tail or something else just as good."

After a while, Mr Rabbit found a garden. He saw an old woman picking lettuce.

"Oh, please, Mr Rabbit," she said, "could I borrow your basket to put my lettuce in?"

"If you give me some of your lettuce," replied Mr Rabbit, "you can keep the basket!" So she did. And off he hopped.

Soon Mr Rabbit felt hungry. He took a bite of the lettuce. It was delicious!

"I've lost my tail and my basket, but I've found something I like much better!" he thought, feeling happy.

The Nightingale

A long, long time ago, Ancient China was ruled by a rich and proud emperor. The emperor loved to be surrounded by fine, expensive objects. The more they glittered with jewels and gold, the happier he was. He had a magnificent palace, filled with priceless treasures, which overlooked the most exquisite gardens.

Talk of the emperor's spectacular palace and gardens spread far and wide. Its beauty was held in such high esteem that many people wrote stories about it. The emperor liked to entertain himself by reading these books. He would sit in his throne room, nodding his approval at each new line of praise. He was a very happy man – until the day he read something that filled his proud heart with jealousy!

In the forest, beyond the emperor's gardens, there lived a tiny brown nightingale. The nightingale loved to sing. Every evening it would warble melodies so beautiful, they filled the heart with happiness.

The emperor hadn't even known of the nightingale's existence or the matchless beauty of its song until that moment.

"Get me the bird! I must hear it sing! How can anything be more beautiful than my palace?" screamed the emperor.

His lord-in-waiting hurried off to find the nightingale.

"Little bird, please come and sing for the emperor," he said.

"It would be an honour," chirped the tiny bird.

Back at the palace, the nightingale sang its glorious song. The tenderness of the melody touched the emperor's heart.

"You must stay and sing for me every day," he cried.

Day after day, the tiny bird sang his magnificent melodies for the emperor. He never complained about being kept in a cage, but he grew sad because he missed the freedom of his forest home.

Then, one day, the emperor received a gift. It was a clockwork nightingale made out of gold and jewels. Its song was beautiful, and the emperor loved his new toy so much that he lost interest in the real nightingale. The little nightingale escaped and flew back to his forest home.

A year went by, and the emperor played his mechanical bird day and night, until finally the toy broke. The emperor was devastated. Now he had no bird to sing to him. He was filled with sadness.

Day after day, he grew weaker and weaker. Then, one evening, as the emperor lay in his bed, close to death, a blissful harmony

suddenly floated in through his open window. It was the nightingale.

"You came back," whispered the emperor. He felt comfort in his heart, and his fever disappeared. "I do not deserve your sweet music. How can I ever repay you?"

"I don't want anything," replied the nightingale. "Knowing that I have touched your heart is enough. I can't come and live in your palace, but I will visit you every evening."

The emperor's face filled with happiness. He realised how foolish and empty his love of riches was. He had been given a second chance, and he vowed to rule his empire wisely from then on.

Surf Frog

Cariad the frog always won the gold medal at the Sandy Beach Surf Contest.

"None of you can beat me," she told the other surfers on the seafront. But, just then, a young frog whizzed towards her on a skateboard. CRASH! The skateboard hurt Cariad's leg.

"Oh no!" cried Cariad. "I won't be able to surf with a sore leg!"

Poor Cariad limped home and shut the door. Her friend Lottie followed her.

"Come back to Sandy Beach to watch the competition with me," Lottie said.

"No, thanks," said Cariad. "If I can't win, I don't want to be there. Winning is all that matters."

But Lottie didn't agree.

"There are lots of young frogs hopping around on the beach with nothing to do," she said. "You could help them."

So, on the first day of the competition, Cariad arrived at Sandy Beach feeling very grumpy. She showed the young frogs how to stand up on a surfboard. They all had a good time, and suddenly Cariad found herself smiling.

Next day, she showed them how to paddle their surfboards in the water.

"You're a great teacher!" said one of the young frogs. Cariad felt proud.

Cariad worked hard to help the young frogs learn to surf.

On the last day of the competition, they put on a surfing show for the crowd. Everyone cheered and clapped, and Cariad was so excited that she forgot all about the competition. The young frogs mattered more than any medal.

"Are you okay?" Lottie asked her, when the medals were handed out.

"I feel great," said Cariad, smiling. "Now I remember how much fun it is just to surf. It's not winning I love. It's surfing!"

Bedtime Adventure

Leah and Megan were not only twin sisters – they were best friends, and they played together all day long.

At bedtime, the twins couldn't wait to wake up and have more fun again in the morning.

One night, as Leah settled down on the top bunk bed, she made a wish upon a star.

"I wish we could play together in our sleep, too," she whispered.

That night, Leah was dreaming of playing with mermaids when, suddenly, she saw Megan flying around the room.

"Are you really flying?" Leah asked, rubbing her eyes.

"Yes," said Megan with a grin. "Come and play!"

Leah jumped out of bed and floated up to the ceiling. Megan took her hand and the window opened, as if by magic.

Together the twins flew out into the sky.

The sisters slid down some moonbeams and dived into the sea. They swam underwater with some fish, while mermaids with silvery tails darted along beside them.

"Let's be mermaids, too," said Leah.

Their legs started to sparkle until they turned into mermaid tails. Leah and Megan flicked and twisted their tails as they followed the mermaids to a big rock. Then they all pulled themselves onto the rock. They ran gem-encrusted combs through their hair, and sang beautiful songs that made dolphins dance in the water below.

Slowly, the stars faded and the sky grew brighter. The night was nearly over… and it was time for the sisters to go home.

Leah opened her eyes and looked down at Megan, who was grinning up at her from the bottom bunk bed.

"Was it all just a dream?" she asked in a whisper.

"Of course," said Megan. "But we both remember it, and I can't wait for our next bedtime adventure!"

The Penny Wise Monkey

Once upon a time, there lived a king who ruled over a rich and prosperous kingdom. But the king was never happy with what he had. He always wanted more.

One day, he set out with his men on yet another mission to take over yet another kingdom. They trekked through the forest all day. By the evening, they were exhausted and stopped to take some rest.

After supper, the soldiers fed their horses apples. In a nearby tree, a hungry monkey watched them. Some of the apples fell on the ground. The monkey jumped down from the tree, grabbed a handful of them, and scampered back up to the top.

As he sat enjoying the apples, one slipped from his hand and fell to the ground. Without thinking, the greedy monkey dropped all the other apples in his hands and ran down to look for the lost apple. He couldn't find it, and climbed back up the tree, empty-handed. His greed made him lose all that he had.

The king, who had been watching the monkey closely, realised that his own need to have more and more might also leave him with nothing one day.

"I will not be like this foolish monkey, who lost so much to gain so little!" he cried. "I will go back to my own kingdom and enjoy what I have."

The Monkeys and the Moon

A long, long time ago, a band of monkeys lived in a forest. In the middle of the forest there was a deep well.

One night, when the leader of the monkeys went to the well to get a drink, he saw the reflection of the moon in the water.

"Oh no!" he gasped. "The moon has fallen in the water. Our sky will have no moon. We must get it out!"

The other monkeys agreed. They formed a chain, each holding onto the tail of the one before them, while the monkey at the top of the chain held on to a branch to support them all.

The branch began to bend under the weight of all the monkeys. Suddenly... CRACK! The branch broke and the monkeys tumbled into the well. The water rippled as they all scrambled to get out of the well, and the reflection of the moon disappeared.

Up above the forest, the moon shone its silvery light on the silly, wet monkeys!

The Gnome

Once upon a time, there was a king who had a special apple tree in his palace garden. The fruit was delicious, but the tree was cursed. The king forbade anyone, including his own three daughters, to eat the apples: if they did, they would find themselves at the bottom of a deep well.

Of course, his daughters couldn't resist the sweet fruits, and they each ate an apple.

In a flash, the three girls disappeared deep underground. When they didn't return home that evening, the king was distraught. He put out a proclamation saying he would offer a huge reward for their safe return.

Three young huntsmen, who were also brothers, set out to look for the princesses. They had been travelling for a few days when they came across a cottage in the forest. There was no sign of anyone living there, and as the two elder brothers didn't like their youngest brother, Hans, they told him to stay at the cottage in case anyone came home. Then they went out to look for the princesses, hoping to get the reward for themselves.

The brothers hadn't been gone long when a strange little gnome appeared in front of Hans. He told the younger brother where the princesses were hidden and how to rescue them.

"The princesses are at the bottom of a deep well in the middle of this forest," explained the gnome. "But go alone because your brothers will betray you."

Hans did as he was told and he soon found the princesses. They were very happy to see him.

That evening, when Hans' brothers returned to the cottage, they were furious to see that Hans had found the princesses himself. So they told Hans to go home, then they took the princesses back to the palace, where they told the king that they had rescued the princesses. But the princesses wanted to thank Hans – their real rescuer – so they told their father the truth.

As punishment, the king banished the two elder brothers from his kingdom for good. Then he rewarded Hans with a huge pot of gold.

And, just to be safe, the king had the apple tree cut down!

Rebecca Rabbit's Birthday Wish

Rebecca Rabbit had just one wish for her birthday. She didn't want presents or even a party.

"Please, please, please," she whispered, "let me have the biggest carrot cake in the world!" But Rebecca was so busy wishing for the cake that she forgot to tell her friends that this was what she really wanted.

On the day of Rebecca's birthday, her friends surprised her with a big party. There were piles of presents and sparkling party hats. But she couldn't see a single cake. Rebecca couldn't help feeling a tiny bit disappointed. She didn't see her friends smiling and winking at each other.

First, Rosie Rabbit held out a very large box. When Rebecca opened it, she found a big cake inside. It was lovely, but it had only one layer.

"Thank you," said Rebecca with a smile.

It wasn't the enormous cake she had dreamed about, but it looked delicious. She knew that Rosie must have worked really hard to bake it.

Then Rex Rabbit held out his present. Rebecca opened it and found another cake, a little smaller than the first.

"I can put it on top of the other cake," she said, starting to feel really excited. Her birthday cake would have two tiers!

One by one, she opened her presents, and each one was a new cake. Hopping with excitement, Rebecca placed them one on top of the other, until the cake was towering above her.

"It really is the biggest carrot cake in the world!" she whispered.

Then, when her friends sang 'Happy Birthday', Rebecca climbed to the top of the cake and blew out her candles. But she didn't make a wish.

"I already have everything I want..." she said happily, "an enormous cake and the greatest friends in the world! Thank you, everyone."

The Lost Shark

Thalia the clownfish and her friends were always being chased by sharks. One day, Thalia saw a baby shark on its own. None of Thalia's friends would help him.

"We don't like sharks," they said.

Thalia felt sorry for the baby. He looked so sad.

Trembling, she whispered, "Are you all right?"

"I've lost my mummy," the baby shark cried.

Thalia had never seen a baby with so many sharp teeth. But she imagined how scared he must feel.

"Come on," she said. "I'll help you find her."

Before long, they found the mummy shark. She had been swimming around, looking for her little one.

"Oh, you've found him," she said to Thalia. Then she bared her teeth... and smiled. Then added, "Thank you!"

Thalia and the baby shark made friends, and Thalia soon found out that the sharks had only been chasing the fish to play.

"Sharks aren't so bad after all!" Thalia said.

Granny's Garden

One day, when Megan visited her granny, no one answered the door. Feeling curious, Megan walked around the side of the house and into the garden. On the grass, she saw half a pumpkin, a spindle, a glass slipper and a mermaid comb. There was even a pot of gold with a rainbow bursting out of it.

"That's odd!" thought Megan. "I've not seen these here before."

Then, all of a sudden, Granny flew across the sky, holding a wand and wearing wings. Megan's mouth fell open.

"You're a fairy godmother!" Megan gasped.

"I'm the fairy godmother," said Granny. "I've just come back from visiting Cinderella, and now I have to dash out for tea with my fairy friends. Next time you visit, I'll tell you all about it. But for now, promise to keep my secret?"

"Of course!" gasped Megan.

Then Granny waved her wand and disappeared in a swirl of sparkles.

Megan couldn't wait for her next trip to Granny's house!

The Wild Swans

Once upon a time, in a distant land, there lived a king. He was blessed with eleven sons and one daughter, Elisa. Sadly, his wife had died. But the king was a loving father and the children were happy.

One day, however, everything changed. The king decided to marry again. His new wife was cruel, but the king was blind to her evil ways. She had Elisa sent away to live with a poor family in the forest, and the princes banished from the kingdom. She cast an enchantment on the boys, transforming them into wild swans. They flew away, wondering sadly if they would ever see their sister again.

The years passed. Elisa was never allowed to return home, and every day her heart ached to see her brothers again.

On her fifteenth birthday, she decided to go in search of the princes.

Elisa walked through the forest until she reached the shores of the ocean. As she gazed at the sun setting below the sea, eleven wild swans landed on the sand. Elisa gasped as the swans suddenly transformed into her brothers.

"Whenever the sun is up, we live as swans," the eldest brother explained. "Only at nightfall may we return to our human form. We live across the ocean now, far away. Come home with us."

So Elisa went to live with her swan brothers.

One night, she had a strange dream. A fairy told her that she must make a nettle shirt for each brother. Once they put it on, the spell would be broken and they would be men again. But Elisa was to stay silent until her work was finished, otherwise her brothers would die.

When Elisa awoke, she started on her task straightaway. She didn't utter a word, even though the nettles stung her hands. She worked hard all day. Just as she was about to return to her brothers, a group of huntsmen, led by a king, appeared.

The king fell in love with Elisa at first sight.

"Come with me to my palace and be my queen," he said.

As Elisa was sworn to silence, she couldn't protest.

Holding the nettle shirts, she reluctantly left with the king.

"Your Majesty, you cannot marry this girl," the archbishop complained. "There is witchcraft at work here, mark my words!"

That night, Elisa tried to sneak out of the palace, but the archbishop caught her and brought her before the king.

"The girl is up to something, Your Majesty," cried the archbishop. "She is a witch!"

The king was heartbroken. Elisa dared not speak to defend herself, and so she was condemned to death.

At sunrise, still clutching the nettle shirts, Elisa was taken to her place of execution. Suddenly, eleven swans swooped down from the sky. Elisa threw the shirts over her swan brothers. They instantly changed into young men.

"Now I may speak," Elisa exclaimed. "I am no witch. All I ever wanted was to break an evil curse and free my brothers."

The king was shocked by this.

"My true love," he cried. "Can you ever forgive me?"

Elisa nodded. The spell had been broken. She had her brothers back, and she knew she would never be unhappy again.

Oscar's Best Surprise

Oscar Bear didn't like surprises. He didn't like trying new foods in case they tasted funny. Or reading new books as he might not like the ending. Or even opening presents... what if he didn't like the gift?

Then, one day, his mother sent him to his friend's house.

"There will be a surprise waiting when you come home," she said.

"I don't like surprises,' Oscar grumbled.

When he arrived, his friend Robyn tried to cheer Oscar up.

"There must be a surprise that you would like," she said.

She showed him a jack-in-the-box. BOING! It sprang up and made Oscar jump. Robyn laughed... but Oscar did not.

"I don't like surprises!" he grumbled.

"Let's play a new game," Robyn said. "How about 'Please, Mr Crocodile'?"

"I don't like new games," said Oscar. "We always play hide-and-seek."

So Oscar and Robyn played hide-and-seek. Oscar always hid in the same place, so the game was over very quickly.

When he got home, his mother waved to him from the window.

"Come in, Oscar!" she called. "The surprise is here."

So Oscar walked into the house. His mother was holding a small, soft bundle.

"Surprise, Oscar," she whispered. "You have a little brother!"

She put the warm bundle into his arms and Oscar gazed down at the tiny baby bear. Two little eyes peeped up at him. Oscar's nose twitched, and then a big smile spread across his face. Maybe some surprises weren't so bad after all.

"You're the best baby bear in the whole world," he whispered. "I can't wait for you to meet my friend Robyn – she'll be so surprised!"

Crocodile Teeth

Chloe Crocodile was getting ready for bedtime. "Will the Tooth Fairy come tonight?" she asked her mummy.

"Your tooth hasn't fallen out yet," her mummy replied, and she kissed Chloe goodnight.

As Chloe lay by the creek, she wobbled her tooth, but it wouldn't budge. Would it ever fall out? Suddenly, a tiny fairy fluttered out from behind a leaf and landed on Chloe's nose.

"I'm Kitty the Tooth Fairy," she said. "Can I help?"

Chloe's mouth fell open in surprise. Kitty reached in and gave the tooth an expert twist and — hey presto! It was out! Kitty put it into her pocket.

"This deserves a very special coin indeed," said Kitty. "Look under your pillow in the morning."

Then Kitty said goodbye and fluttered away as quickly as she had appeared.

The next day, Chloe found a crocodile coin under her pillow, with a little note that said: 'Even crocodiles have visits from the Tooth Fairy.' Chloe couldn't wait to show her mummy!

The Stone Soup

Samuel was on his way to visit a friend, but he was cold, tired and hungry. Up ahead, he saw a little cottage.

"Please could you spare me some food?" he asked the owner of the cottage.

"I don't have any," lied the old woman.

"Could I borrow your pot and cook some tasty soup?" Samuel asked.

"You may, if you share it with me," replied the old woman.

So Samuel filled the pot with water. Then he found two large stones outside. He cleaned them and put them in the pot.

"What kind of soup are you making?" asked the old woman in surprise.

"Stone soup," replied Samuel. "It's wonderful, but it would taste even better with some vegetables."

"I've got carrots and potatoes," the old woman said.

Samuel added the vegetables and stirred the soup.

Then he said, "With seasoning, it would be perfect!"

"I've got salt and pepper," replied the old woman.

Soon the soup was ready. "Hmm, delicious," said the old woman, not realising she was sharing her food after all!

Bird Bear

Isla was a little bear cub. She lived in the woods with her mummy and daddy, and her big sister. One day, she was playing with her sister when she saw some blue tits swooping out of their nest, high up in a tree. Isla stared at the birds as they glided and fluttered and flew. Then she gave a deep, long sigh.

"I want to fly like that," she said.

"Bears can't fly," said her sister.

"Then I don't want to be a bear any more," Isla said. "I want to be a blue tit and fly through the sky, and live in a nest in a tree."

Isla's sister just shook her head. She knew that bears couldn't turn into birds. But Isla couldn't stop thinking about it. She climbed up the tree and watched the birds all afternoon. Her sister got fed up and wandered off, but Isla didn't care.

"Birds have wings," she said to herself. "If I make myself some wings, maybe I'll be able to fly too."

She pulled two leafy branches off the tree and climbed down. Holding one in each hand, Isla started to run, flapping the branches up and down as fast as she could. But she didn't raise a single toe off the ground. Feeling gloomy, she walked back towards home, trailing the branches behind her.

On the way, Isla spotted a finch pecking the ground. As she watched, the finch pulled a worm out of the ground and swallowed it whole. Then it flew away.

"Hmm," said Isla. "Perhaps I need to learn to be a bird in other ways before I can fly."

She dropped the branches and knelt down on the ground. After a long wait, she saw a worm poking through the soil. With a single gulp, she swallowed it down. It tasted horrible!

"Yuck!" she growled. "Yuck! Yuck! Yuck! Why do birds eat worms? Someone should tell them about honey!"

Just then, a blackbird nearby started to sing.

"That's it!" Isla exclaimed. "I will learn to sing as sweetly as a bird!"

She opened her mouth as wide as it would go, and began to sing in her highest voice.

"ARRRGHHH! EEEEEE! OOOOOOH!" All the animals nearby dived for cover. The birds shot up out of the trees in fright. A rabbit poked her head out of a hole in the ground and glared at Isla.

"Stop making that awful noise!" she snapped. "My babies are asleep!"

"I'm sorry," said Isla. "I was trying to sing like a bird."

"Well, it didn't work," said the rabbit in a cross voice. "If I were you, I'd stop trying to be something you're not."

Suddenly, Isla felt very tired. She was about to sit down for a rest when she saw her mummy gathering honeycombs for supper. She clambered onto her mummy's back and held on tight.

"What a tired bear," said her mummy. "Have you had a busy day?"

"Very busy," said Isla, yawning. "Mummy, why can't I be a bird and fly around?"

"Because you're a bear cub, and that's what you do best," said her mummy. "Now, shall I carry you home and tell you all about the trees we're going to climb tomorrow? I know where to find all the biggest honeycombs."

Isla nodded and snuggled into her mummy's cosy fur.

Night started to fall, and the moon came out. Isla yawned again. She still thought that being able to fly like a bird would be wonderful. But being able to climb trees and eat honeycombs with her mummy was even better!

Cleo and the Unicorn

Cleo dreamed of meeting a unicorn.

"They don't exist," said Cleo's mum.

"You're being silly," said her brother.

Even her dad smiled and patted her on the head.

One day, Cleo was playing in the garden when she heard a snorting noise behind the shed. She went to find out what it was and saw a small, muddy animal.

"Hello," said Cleo in a gentle voice. "What are you?" She carefully picked up the creature. "You're a tiny pony!" she exclaimed. "Let me clean you up, little one."

Cleo bathed the pony in her paddling pool. Underneath all the dirt, the pony was as white as snow. Cleo wrapped it in her best fleecy blanket and read it a story until it fell asleep. Then she looked up and gasped in surprise. A shining white unicorn was standing beside the shed!

"I've always wanted to see a unicorn," whispered Cleo.

"You already have," said the unicorn with a smile. "You are cuddling my baby. I have been searching for him all day."

"But he doesn't have a horn," said Cleo.

"Unicorn horns don't grow until we're older," said the unicorn. "Thank you for taking care of him."

Cleo unfolded the blanket and the little unicorn woke up. He trotted happily to his mummy.

"Will I ever see him again?" Cleo asked.

"Because you took care of my baby, a tiny bit of unicorn magic will stay with you," the unicorn said. "If you are ever in trouble, we will come to help you."

"Thank you," gasped Cleo happily.

The unicorn flicked her mane, and left in a swirl of silver sparkles. Cleo couldn't stop smiling. She had met a real unicorn, and found that wishes do come true.

103

The Enormous Pancake

Once upon a time, there was a woman who had seven little boys. They were always hungry.

"If you are very good," said their mother, "I will make you the biggest pancake you have ever seen!"

So she cracked the eggs, measured the milk, weighed the flour and mixed it all together. Then she poured the mixture into a hot pan. The pancake was going to be enormous!

When it was time to flip it over, the hungry little boys cried out, "Toss it in the air, Mother, please!"

So their mother tossed the pancake high into the air.

But the pancake didn't want to be eaten, so with a flip and a flop it landed on the floor and rolled out of the door.

"Stop!" cried the hungry little boys. "We want to eat you!"

But the pancake didn't want to be eaten. So it rolled down the road, with the boys and their mother chasing after it.

Soon, the pancake passed a cat.

"Stop!" miaowed the cat, licking her lips. "You would taste yummy washed down with a bowl of milk. Let me eat you."

But the pancake just rolled faster. "Seven little boys and their mother couldn't catch me, and you won't either!" it shouted. So the cat chased after it.

Next, the pancake passed a duck pond.

"Stop!" quacked the duck. "I prefer pancakes to stale bread, so I'm going to eat you up!"

But the pancake rolled even faster. "Seven little boys, their mother and a cat couldn't catch me, and you won't either!" So the duck chased after it.

Then, the pancake passed a cow in a field.

"Stop!" mooed the cow. "I'll eat you instead of this grass!"

But the pancake rolled even faster still. "Seven little boys, their mother, a cat and a duck couldn't catch me, and you won't either!" So the cow chased after it.

Soon, the pancake met a pig by a river.

"Can you help me cross the river?" asked the pancake.

"Of course!" snorted the pig. "Sit on my nose and I'll carry you across." So the pancake jumped onto his nose.

In a flash, the pig flipped the pancake into the air and gobbled it up in one enormous GULP! "Yum!" said the pig.

Just then, the seven little boys, their mother, the cat, the duck and the cow arrived.

"Have you seen an enormous pancake?" they asked.

"Yes," snorted the pig happily, "and it was delicious!"

Androclus and the Lion

A long time ago in Rome, there lived a poor slave whose name was Androclus. His master was a cruel man, and Androclus wished that he could be free.

One night, Androclus managed to escape. He ran away and hid in a cave outside the city.

Androclus was so tired, cold and hungry that he fell into a deep sleep. A while later, a great noise woke him up. A lion had come into the cave and was roaring loudly. At first, Androclus feared that the lion would eat him. But then he realised that the lion was limping in pain.

Boldly, Androclus took the lion's paw in his hand to see what was wrong. A large thorn was poking out of the lion's pad. Androclus removed the thorn gently. The lion was so grateful that he licked Androclus' face!

After this, Androclus and the lion became the best of friends and lived happily together in the cave.

Several months later, some soldiers were passing nearby. They found Androclus and took him back to Rome.

At that time, it was the law that any slave who'd run away, and was caught, had to fight a hungry lion for their freedom.

Poor Androclus was put in an arena to await his fate. He closed his eyes in fear as a hungry lion ran towards him. But instead of being attacked, the lion licked Androclus' face!

Androclus gave a cry of joy. It was his old friend the lion from the cave. He put his arms around the huge beast and hugged it in gratitude.

The crowd were astounded – they had never seen anything like this before. They called out to Androclus to explain what had happened.

"I am a man," Androclus cried. "But no man has ever been kind to me. This magnificent lion is the closest thing I've ever had to a friend. We love each other like brothers."

The crowd were so moved by Androclus' story that they chanted, "Let him live and be free! And let the lion go, too!"

And from then on, Androclus and the lion lived happily together in Rome.

Daisy and the Genie

Daisy bought an old tin lamp at a jumble sale.

"It just needs a quick polish and it will look as good as new again," she decided.

But when Daisy rubbed the lamp with a cloth, there was a loud bang and a puff of smoke. A small boy appeared with his arms folded across his chest.

"I am a genie!" he said. "I grant you three wishes!"

"Wow!" said Daisy. "How long have you been in the lamp?"

"I've been trapped for ages," the little genie admitted. "I'm training to be a genie. I was waiting for someone to rub the lamp and say their wishes, so I could return to Genie School."

"Can you really give me three wishes?" Daisy asked.

The genie nodded. "They might go wrong," he warned her. "I'm still learning. That's why I need to go back home."

"I wish for a new swing," Daisy began.

The genie snapped his fingers and a shiny new spring appeared in Daisy's hand.

"Oops!" said the genie. "That wasn't supposed to happen."

"Let's try something else," said Daisy with a laugh. "I wish for a house made of chocolate!"

Once again, the genie snapped his fingers and a large chocolate mouse appeared in Daisy's other hand.

"Oh dear," said the genie, sadly. "I'm not doing very well."

Daisy felt sorry for the little genie. She tried again.

"I wish for... a pet dog," she said finally.

The genie snapped his fingers and a frog appeared in Daisy's pocket. Daisy laughed, then noticed the genie was fading away.

"Where are you going?" she cried.

"I'm going back to Genie School," said the genie. "When a human makes three wishes, I can return. Thank you, Daisy!"

The genie and the lamp disappeared in a puff of smoke. Daisy looked at the spring, the chocolate mouse and the frog, and she smiled.

"You're welcome," she whispered.

Princess Elodie's Wish Hunt

Princess Elodie lived in Cloudland, and every day she chose which one of her beautiful cloud ponies she wanted to ride. Then she galloped around her kingdom to collect the wishes of children who had wished upon a star.

One morning, she found it very hard to decide which pony to ride. Should she choose Locket with her golden mane, or Emerald with her sparkling green eyes? The cloud ponies were all so beautiful. Then she heard a soft whinny and turned around. Behind her was a white pony with a curly mane that was as soft as the clouds.

"Hello, Cobweb," said Princess Elodie. "Would you like to go for a ride this morning?"

Cobweb whinnied again, so Princess Elodie fetched a saddle of blue satin.

"Let's go wish-hunting!" she said.

With Princess Elodie on his back, Cobweb galloped over the fluffy cloud hills and through the soft cloud meadows. Wishes were easy to spot because they looked like flowers, and the cloud bunnies loved to chase them.

Princess Elodie scooped up the wishes and put them in her pocket.

Just then, she spotted something half hidden among the cloud blossoms. After telling Cobweb to wait, she slipped down and brushed the blossoms aside. A little brown teddy was lying there, looking very sad.

"Poor lost teddy," said Princess Elodie, cuddling him tightly. "I'll look after you."

Cobweb carried Princess Elodie and the teddy back to the Cloud Palace. After Princess Elodie had removed the blue satin saddle and given Cobweb some food, she took the teddy into the palace. First she mended a tear along his arm and then she washed him and sat him beside the roaring fire to dry.

"Now," she said. "What shall I do with you?"

She emptied her pockets and the wishes spilled out over the palace floor. There were wishes for dolls, sunny days, fairgrounds and lots more, but Princess Elodie was looking for a very special wish. It took a long time to sort through and grant all the wishes, but at last she found what she was looking for. A lonely little boy had wished for a teddy bear friend.

Smiling, Princess Elodie went to fetch Cobweb. By the time she had brushed him down and saddled him, the teddy was dry. Princess Elodie tucked him under her arm, climbed onto Cobweb and held up the little boy's wish.

"Take us to the child who made this wish, please," she said.

Cobweb neighed and walked to the edge of Cloudland. A puffy cloud started to change shape, forming a set of steps that wound down through the night sky. Cobweb trotted down the cloud steps, while Elodie waved to the stars that twinkled all around them. The steps led them all the way to the little boy's bedroom window.

"Shhh," said Princess Elodie. She slipped off Cobweb's back onto the windowsill. Then she opened the window and stepped inside. The little boy was fast asleep in his bed, so Princess Elodie tucked the teddy into bed beside him. In his sleep, the boy smiled and put his arm around the teddy.

"Time to go," said Princess Elodie.

She climbed out of the window and back onto Cobweb. Then he carried her up to Cloudland, where her swinging bed was hanging from the moon.

Yawning, Princess Elodie took Cobweb's saddle off and gave him a blanket and some food. Then she climbed onto her swing and drifted off to sleep, dreaming of the teddy and his happy new home.

Little Rabbit's Big Adventure!

Little Rabbit sat still in the tall grass. He glanced all around, but nothing looked familiar. Mummy Rabbit had told him not to go too far from the burrow. But, being a curious little bunny, he'd forgotten her words as soon as he'd seen the little buzzing bee fly by and had decided to follow it. Now he didn't know where he was.

"Oh no! I'm lost," cried Little Rabbit. "How will I get home?"

He looked around again. A beautiful pink butterfly was fluttering around some flowers nearby.

"Hello, Mrs Butterfly," called Little Rabbit. "I'm lost. Do you know where my burrow is?"

"Sorry, I don't," said the butterfly. "Try asking the sheep in that field."

"That's a good idea," replied Little Rabbit. He hopped off through the flowers and squeezed under a fence.

"Hello, Mrs Sheep," said Little Rabbit, "do you know where my burrow is?"

"No, I'm sorry, my dear," baaed the sheep.

Tears started to slide down Little Rabbit's face. "I miss my mummy, and I want to go home!"

"Don't cry," a squirrel called out from a tree at the edge of the field. "I know where your burrow is. Follow me."

"Oh, thank you, Mr Squirrel!" said Little Rabbit.

Little Rabbit followed the squirrel into the woods. After a little while the squirrel stopped.

"Here we are!" he said.

And there was Mummy Rabbit, standing by a small dark hole at the base of a big tree.

"Little Rabbit!" cried Mummy Rabbit, scooping him into her arms. "Where have you been? I've been so worried."

Little Rabbit told Mummy Rabbit all about his big adventure.

"What a brave bunny you are!" said Mummy.

Little Rabbit smiled and snuggled closer to his mummy. "But it's good to be back home."

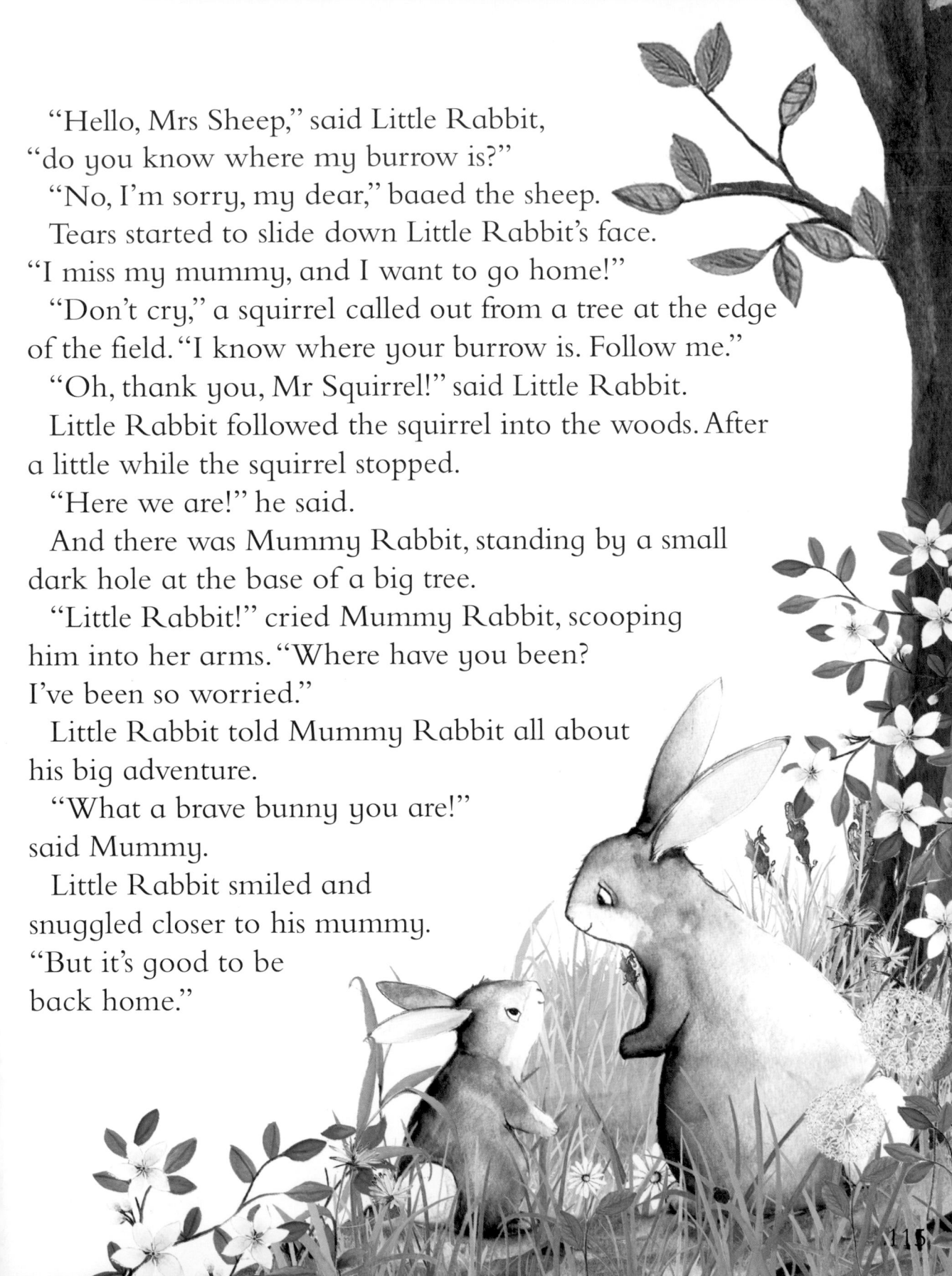

The Loudest ROAR!

Leo the little lion cub wanted to be just like Daddy when he grew up.

"I'm going to have the loudest ROAR ever!" he said.

Daddy Lion grinned and patted Leo gently on the head with his large paw.

"Yes, one day you will," he said. "But while you are still little, why don't we go and play?"

"Teach me to roar like you first, Daddy, please!" pleaded Leo. He opened his little mouth but...

"GRRRRR!"

Leo could only make a tiny growling sound. The little lion cub stomped his paws on the ground in frustration.

"It needs to be louder, Daddy!" he cried.

Daddy lion smiled. "Don't worry, Leo, it will get louder with practice." Then he opened his mouth wide...

"RRRRRRROAR!"

The roar was so loud that the ground trembled under Leo's paws!

"GRRRRR!" Leo tried again.

"Sit up straight and tip your head back," advised Daddy. "And then open your mouth as wide as it will go…"

116

Leo watched Daddy lion closely. He sat up straight, tipped his head back and opened his mouth as wide as it would go...

"RRRRRROAR!"

Leo could feel the ground trembling under his paws.

"That's my boy!" laughed Daddy. "You've got it!"

Leo was so happy with his new roar that he practised it all afternoon. Soon he was exhausted.

"That's enough for today," said Daddy as he settled Leo down for bed. "You don't want to lose your voice."

But Leo didn't hear him. He was already fast asleep, dreaming about his wonderful new loud roar!

Darcie's Treasure

Darcie's uncle was a treasure hunter. He used a special metal detector to search for riches.

One day, Darcie lost her necklace in the garden. So she asked her uncle if he could help her find it.

"Once, I discovered old coins and a medieval queen's jewellery in your garden," he told Darcie. "Legend says that she left a priceless golden goblet here too, but it's probably just a story."

Then Darcie's uncle showed her how to use the metal detector. When they reached the end of the garden, it beeped. Darcie and her uncle started to dig. They found a dirty old cup. When Darcie washed it, she saw that it was gold with red rubies around the side.

"The queen's goblet!" gasped her uncle.

Then the metal detector beeped again. This time they found Darcie's necklace. "You're going to be the best treasure hunter ever, Darcie!" said her uncle, with a grin.

Magic Museum

Zara loved the costume museum. She was fascinated by the clothes people wore hundreds of years ago, and the things they used in their homes. Best of all, she loved imagining that she lived in the old days too.

One day, during a visit, the guide asked Zara if she'd like to try something on. Feeling excited, Zara dressed up in a kitchen maid's uniform. Suddenly, the room around her disappeared and she found herself in a kitchen full of busy maids and butlers.

"Hurry up!" shouted the cook. "Don't dawdle!"

At first, Zara helped the cook prepare the food. But soon she was washing dishes and scrubbing floors. It was hard work! As Zara bent down, her cap fell off. And in a twinkling, the servants and the kitchen vanished. Zara was back in the museum.

"Will you come back tomorrow?" asked the guide.

"Yes, please. But I think a princess dress might suit me better!" said Zara, thinking about the kitchen from long ago.

Rapunzel

Once upon a time, a poor young couple lived in a cottage next door to an old witch. The witch grew many vegetables in her garden, but she kept them all for herself.

One day, the couple had only a few potatoes left to eat.

"Surely it wouldn't matter if we took just a few vegetables," said the wife, gazing longingly over the wall.

So her husband quickly climbed into the garden and started to fill his basket. Suddenly he heard an angry voice.

"How dare you steal my vegetables?"

"Please don't hurt me," begged the young man. "My wife is going to have a baby soon, and she is hungry!"

"You may keep the vegetables," she croaked. "But you must give me the baby when it is born."

Terrified, the man had to agree.

Months later, his wife gave birth to a little girl. And although the parents begged and cried, the cruel witch took the baby. She called her Rapunzel.

Years passed and Rapunzel grew up to be kind and beautiful. The witch was so afraid of losing her that she built a tall tower with no door and only one window. She planted thorn bushes all around it, then she locked Rapunzel in the tower.

Each day, Rapunzel brushed and combed her long golden locks. And each day, the witch came to visit her, standing at the foot of the tower and calling out, "Rapunzel, Rapunzel, let down your hair."

Rapunzel hung her hair out of the window and the witch climbed up it to sit and talk with her. But Rapunzel was very lonely. She sat at her window and sang sadly.

One day, a prince rode by and heard the beautiful singing coming from the witch's garden. As he hid behind the wall, he saw the old witch call out, "Rapunzel, Rapunzel, let down your hair."

The prince saw a cascade of golden hair fall from the tower, and he watched the witch climb up it.

When the witch returned to her house, he crept to the tower. "Rapunzel, Rapunzel, let down your hair," he called softly.

Rapunzel let down her locks and the prince climbed up.

Rapunzel was very surprised to see the prince, and delighted when he said he wanted to be her friend. From then on, the prince came to visit her every day.

Months passed and Rapunzel and the prince fell in love.

"How can we be together?" Rapunzel cried. "The witch will never let me go."

So the prince brought some silk which Rapunzel knotted together to make a ladder so that she could escape from the tower.

One day, without thinking, Rapunzel remarked to the witch, "It's much harder to pull you up than the prince!"

The witch was furious! "What prince?" she shouted.

She grabbed Rapunzel's long hair and cut it off. Then she used her magic to send Rapunzel far into the forest.

That evening, when the prince came to see Rapunzel, the witch held the golden hair out of the window and he climbed up into the tower, coming face to face with the old witch.

"You will never see Rapunzel again!" she screamed, and pushed the prince out of the window. He fell into the thorn bushes below. The sharp spikes scratched his eyes and blinded him. Weeping, he stumbled away.

After months of wandering, blind and lost, the prince heard beautiful, sad singing floating through the woods. He recognised Rapunzel's voice and called out to her.

"At last I have found you!" she cried. As her tears fell into the prince's eyes, his wounds healed, and he could see again.

Rapunzel had never been so happy. She and the prince were soon married, and they lived happily ever after, far away from the old witch and her empty tower.

The Clever Monkey

One day, Tiger was prowling through the jungle, looking for his lunch. He was just about to pounce on an unsuspecting deer, when his legs became trapped in a tangle of vines.

Poor Tiger was trying to think of a way to escape the trap, when he saw the deer he'd been hoping to eat for his lunch.

"Please help me, Deer!" he cried loudly. "Untangle the vines to set me free!"

Trembling, Deer shook her head.

"You'll eat me if I set you free."

"I promise I won't," said Tiger. "We can be friends."

Deer thought it would be better to have Tiger as a friend, rather than an enemy, so she untangled the vines.

But as soon as Tiger was free, he pounced on Deer.

"You promised not to eat me!" pleaded Deer.

"But I'm hungry!" roared Tiger.

Deer started to sob.

"What's going on?" asked Monkey, who was passing nearby. He'd heard Deer crying.

"Monkey," sniffed Deer, "do you think it is right for Tiger to eat me when I have just saved his life?"

"You did not save my life!" roared Tiger.

"Well, tigers do usually like to eat deer," replied Monkey. "Tiger, why don't you show me where you were, and then I can see if Deer really saved your life."

Grumbling to himself, Tiger let Deer tie the vines around his legs to show Monkey where he had been trapped.

Quick as a flash, Monkey jumped onto Deer's back.

"Come on, Deer," he chuckled. "Let's go!"

"Thanks, Monkey," said Deer. "Now you've saved my life!"

Tiger roared loudly as he found himself trapped once more.

The Golden Goose

There was once a man who had three sons. Two of them were clever, but everyone thought the youngest, called Peter, was silly.

One day, the father sent the eldest son, Luke, into the forest to chop down a tree. He was just about to start work when a little old man appeared.

"Please can I have some food?" the old man asked.

"If I give some to you, there won't be much for me," Luke replied. Then he began to chop down the tree.

As if by magic, the eldest son's axe slipped and he cut his arm, so he had to go home.

As the wood still needed chopping, the father sent the middle son, Paul, into the forest. Once again, the little old man appeared.

"Please can I have some food?" asked the old man.

But the middle son refused. "I won't have much left if I give some to you," he replied.

Suddenly, Paul's axe slipped and he cut his leg. So he had to go home, too.

"Father, let me chop down the tree," said Peter.

His father laughed. "What makes you think you can do it if your brothers can't?"

But Peter begged his father until he gave in.

Peter set off to the forest. It wasn't long before he met the little old man.

"Please can I have some food?" asked the old man.

"There's not much," Peter said. "But you are welcome to share it with me."

"You're a kind boy," said the old man, as they sat down to eat. "Let me give you something in return."

The old man told Peter to cut down the tree and see what was inside its roots.

Peter did as the old man said. Inside the roots was a goose with golden feathers. Puzzled, Peter looked around for the old man, but he had mysteriously disappeared.

By now it was getting late, so Peter picked up the goose and went to find an inn for the night.

The inn-keeper had three daughters and they were fascinated by the goose's golden feathers. One by one, they reached out to pluck a golden feather, but the moment they touched the bird, they stuck to the goose and couldn't let go!

In the morning, the girls were still stuck to the goose. So Peter set out for home, with the three girls trailing behind him.

When other people saw the strange procession, they tried to pull the girls free, only to become stuck too!

Peter's journey took him through a city ruled by a king. The king's daughter was so sad and the king couldn't make her happy. In desperation, he offered her hand in marriage to anyone who could make her laugh.

As soon as the princess saw Peter's ridiculous procession, she began to laugh as if she would never stop.

The king was thrilled. "You may marry my daughter!" he told Peter.

So Peter and the princess soon married. They lived a happy life, full of laughter, and no one made fun of Peter any more.

I Want to Be TALL!

Delilah was a little dinosaur. She lived in a cosy cave with her mum and dad and had a happy life. But there was one thing Delilah wished for more than anything else…

She wanted to be TALL!

"It's not fair!" cried Delilah, stamping her little feet. "I can't reach the juicy fruits and leaves at the tops of the trees."

"You will be able to one day, Delilah," soothed Mummy. "You just have to wait to grow up."

"But I want to be tall NOW!" roared Delilah crossly. "I want to be taller than the trees."

"You might bump your head on the ceiling if you get that tall!" laughed Daddy.

"Better than being this small," Delilah thought grumpily to herself. Surely there must be a way of getting taller quicker.

Delilah tried jumping high into the sky.

She tried stretching her arms up.

She even ate all her vegetables, because Mummy said they would make her grow big and strong.

But nothing seemed to work.

One evening, Delilah went for a walk
with Daddy.

"I wish I was tall enough to reach the stars!"
sighed Delilah. "If only I was taller than…"

RRRRRROAR!

"What's that?" screamed Delilah, as a giant creature
came rushing out of the trees.

"Run, Delilah!" shouted Daddy. "It's a Tyrannosaurus Rex!"

As Delilah dashed after Daddy, she spied a small opening in
the rocky cliff up ahead.

"Daddy, quick! Let's hide in here," cried Delilah.

Delilah and Daddy squeezed into the small dark cave.

Outside, the huge T-Rex roared in frustration. He
was too tall to fit through the gap in the rocks.

Daddy hugged Delilah close. "Well done,
Delilah – you saved us!"

Delilah grinned up at Daddy.

"Perhaps being small isn't so bad after
all," she laughed.

Small World

Elizabeth and Jamie were best friends, and they loved playing together in the woods behind their homes.

One day, when they were in Jamie's front garden, Jamie saw a little grasshopper on the pavement outside. He picked him up with gentle hands.

"You might get trodden on if you stay there," Jamie told him. "We'll help you. We know how it feels to be small."

So Jamie and Elizabeth put the little grasshopper on some grass at the side of the pavement.

"Thank you," said the grasshopper. "You are very kind."

Jamie couldn't believe his ears. His mouth fell open in amazement.

"You can talk!" he exclaimed.

"All animals can talk," said the grasshoppers. "We just don't choose to talk to humans very often. Would you like to come to the woods with me? I will take you to the Land of Animals. No human has ever visited it before!"

"We'd love to," said Elizabeth.

The grasshopper jumped ahead of them and they ran down the path behind him, giggling as they chased the little green creature into the woods.

They ran and jumped over bracken and logs, until the grasshopper stopped beside a small green leaf. It had a hole in the middle of it. The grasshopper tapped the leaf with one of his wings, and the leaf grew until the hole was the size of a door. The grasshopper turned and smiled at them.

"Welcome to my home!" he said.

He hopped through the hole, and the children followed him.

Everything was different through the hole. The sky was bluer. The grass was greener. Even the sun shone a little more brightly. Best of all, everywhere the children looked, they saw animals. Everyone was playing happily. Butterflies danced together, making beautiful patterns and shapes with their wings. Bunnies hopped around them, and birds landed on their shoulders, singing their merriest songs.

"Look at the ladybirds!" cried Elizabeth. They were looping the loop and twisting and diving through the air.

Tiny brown bunny rabbits hopped around the trees, playing catch and hide-and-seek. When they saw the children, they stopped and waved their paws.

"Come and play with us!" they called.

Elizabeth and Jamie could hardly wait! They followed the rabbits as they bounded around the trees, and ran deeper into the Land of Animals.

The children hid among flowering bushes, and the rabbits looked for them, thumping their big feet in delight when they won.

Elizabeth and Jamie made friends with speckled deer, and climbed trees with the squirrels to look for nuts. Finally, the light faded, and owls peered out from trees with sleepy eyes.

"Time to go home," they hooted. "The grasshopper will be waiting for you."

Elizabeth and Jamie hurried back to the leaf with the big hole in it. The grasshopper was there, right beside the magical leaf.

"Did you have a good time?" he asked.

"It's been the most amazing day ever," said Elizabeth. "We've loved every moment."

"And we've loved having you visit the Land of Animals," the grasshopper replied. "You are very special. Not many humans remember how it feels to be small."

"We will never forget," said Jamie as they stepped back through the magical leaf door. "We promise!"

Unicorn Magic

Once upon a time, there were two little unicorns called Lottie and Lulu, and they lived with their mother in a cave on top of a mountain.

Unicorns are magical creatures and their twisty horns are full of spells and enchantments. But little unicorns have to learn how to use their magic… and they don't always get it right!

One day, Lottie and Lulu's mother went to visit some friends. As soon as she had trotted out of sight, Lottie and Lulu shared a big smile.

"Let's give her a surprise," said Lottie. "Let's magically tidy up the cave."

Lottie said the first spell, and purple sparkles flew out of her twisty horn and hit a messy heap of hay in the corner. But instead of tidying it up, the spell turned the hay purple.

"Let me try," said Lulu. As she said her spell, green sparkles zipped out of her twisty horn and hit a bowl of apples. They turned into beetles and scuttled off.

"Let's do the dusting," said Lottie. She tried to make the dust vanish, but it turned into a cloud of glitter instead.

"Oh no! What a mess," gasped Lulu.

Things got worse and worse. Every spell that Lottie and Lulu tried went wrong. They made their beds with honey instead of heather. They covered the ceiling with blue cornflowers. They turned the ribbons that their mother decorated her mane with into butterflies.

And that was when their mother came back.

"Oh dear," she said, looking around at the chaos.

"We're sorry," said Lulu. "We were trying to help, but every spell went wrong."

Their mother nuzzled them both.

"It's all right," she said. "It is a bit messy, but I don't think I have ever seen the cave looking so pretty and colourful!"

Princess Bea's Wish

Princess Bea didn't like getting messy. She would rather play in her bedroom, where everything was neat and tidy, than go outside and get muddy.

Then, on Bea's birthday, her fairy godmother gave her three magic wishes.

"Thank you!" Princess Bea said. "My first two wishes are a doll's house and a toy puppy."

Bea's fairy godmother waved her wand and, with a tinkle of silver bells, the new toys magically appeared.

Bea started playing with them, but they weren't as much fun as she had hoped.

"I'm bored of playing indoors," she thought.

So she went for a ride in her carriage. Soon she saw the village children sitting by the stream, looking sad. Bea stopped the carriage and got out.

"What's wrong?" she asked them.

"The rope swing over the stream has broken," said one of the children. "We've got nothing to play on."

Bea thought hard. She had lots of toys. She didn't really need her third wish.

"I wish for the rope swing to be repaired," she whispered.

Suddenly, there was a magical flash and lots of rope swings appeared over the river. The children squealed in delight.

"Come and play with us!" they called to Bea.

Bea thought it might be fun, so she did.

138

Later, when the princess went home, her dress was torn, her knees were muddy and her hair was full of brambles. She had even lost one of her shoes!

"What a messy princess!" said her fairy godmother, smiling. "Did you have a good time?"

"Yes, thank you," said Bea. "Today was the best birthday ever! I had so much fun with my new friends, I forgot all about getting messy."

Poorly Bunny

Bunny did not feel well. Her little twitchy nose felt all snuffly.

"ATISHOO!" she sneezed loudly.

"Oh, my poor little bunny," said her mummy. "I think you've caught a cold."

So Mummy gently tucked Bunny up in bed.

"You need to rest and stay warm," she told her.

"But I don't want to!" sniffled Bunny. "I want to go outside and play!"

Mummy wiped Bunny's sneezy nose and kissed her softly on her fluffy ears.

"Snuggle under your covers and go to sleep now. I'll come and check on you in a little while," she said, as she quietly closed the bedroom door.

But as soon as Mummy had gone, Bunny got out of bed. Her legs felt wobbly and her body ached.

"Come on, Teddy, let's go!" she told her cuddly toy. "We're going outside!"

Shaking and shivering, Bunny slowly crawled downstairs. She was just reaching for the front door handle when Mummy suddenly appeared behind her.

"Bunny!" Mummy scolded. "Where are you going?"

Then Mummy scooped Bunny up into her warm arms and carried her into the lounge.

"Let's snuggle up on the sofa and I'll read you a story," she said softly. "Then, if you feel a bit better, you can go outside."

Bunny smiled and hugged her mummy tightly.

"Thank you," she sighed.

But as Mummy started to read Bunny's favourite book, Bunny's eyes began to feel heavy, and her ears flopped forward.

It was warm and cosy next to Mummy and before long, Bunny was fast asleep.

"Sweet dreams, my little one," Mummy whispered, and she gently carried Bunny back to her bed.

Hazel's Comforter

Hazel loved her comforter. It was made of moss as soft as her mummy's coat, and she always kept it with her. But, one day, after she had been playing in the forest, her comforter vanished.

"Where is it?" she cried. "I can't sleep without it."

She searched the leafy forest floor. She searched the low branches of trees. It was no use – her comforter was gone.

"Borrow mine," said Squirrel. But Squirrel's comforter was too bushy.

"Borrow mine," said Hedgehog. But Hedgehog's comforter was too prickly. Hazel went to bed feeling miserable.

"Don't be sad," said her mummy. "We'll find you a new comforter tomorrow. But, tonight, snuggle up to me. I will stay with you all night long."

Hazel smiled, closed her eyes and fell fast asleep. After all, no one needs a comforter when they have a mummy cuddle!

Rainbow Farm

Isla's fairy wand had a mind of its own. One day, while Isla was asleep, her wand came to life. POOF! Full of magical mischief, it flew out of Fairyland, looking for fun. The first thing it saw was a farm. FlASH! The pigs turned purple. WHOOSH! The trees went turquoise. SWISH! The sheep became scarlet.

"This is crazy!" neighed a pink pony.

"What's happened?" clucked a rainbow-coloured hen.

Just then, Isla appeared. She had followed the trail of fairy dust. "Naughty wand, return to me!" she exclaimed. "Turn things back how they should be!"

At once, everything returned to normal. But the animals didn't look very happy.

"I loved my gold spots," wailed the cockerel.

"I miss my blue tail," sniffed the cow.

"Can you change us back again?" the animals begged.

Isla laughed. And now animals come from far and wide to visit the most colourful farm in the world!

Puss in Boots

There was once an old miller who had three sons. When the miller died, he left the mill to his oldest son. The middle son was given the donkeys. The youngest son, a kind man who had always put his father and brothers before himself, was left nothing but his father's cat.

"What will become of me?" sighed the miller's young son, looking at his cat.

"Buy me a fine pair of boots and I will help you make your fortune, just as your father had wished," replied the cat.

A talking cat! The miller's son could not believe his ears.

He bought the cat a fine pair of boots and the two of them set off to seek their fortune.

After a while, they came to a grand palace.

"I wish I could live so grandly," sighed the miller's son.

Later, the cat went hunting and caught a rabbit. He put it in a sack and took it to the king.

"A gift from my master, the Marquis of Carabas," said the cat, pretending the miller's son was a grand nobleman.

"Now the king will want to know all about you," laughed the cat, when he told his master what he had done.

The cat delivered gifts all that week, and the king became very curious. So much so, he decided his daughter should meet this mysterious Marquis of Carabas.

The clever cat rushed back to his master, telling him to take off all his clothes and stand in the river by the side of the road.

The puzzled miller's son did as he was told and the cat quickly hid his master's tattered clothes behind a rock.

When the cat heard the king's carriage coming, he jumped out into the road.

"Your Majesty," cried the cat, "my master's clothes were stolen while he was bathing in the river."

The king gave the miller's son a suit of fine clothes to wear and invited him into the carriage.

The miller's son looked very handsome in his new suit and the king's daughter fell in love with him at once.

Meanwhile, the cat quickly ran on ahead. Every time he met people working in the fields, he told them, "If the king stops to ask who owns this land, you must tell him it belongs to the Marquis of Carabas."

Beyond the fields, the cat reached a grand castle belonging to a fierce ogre. The cat bravely knocked on the door and called out, "I have heard that you are a very clever ogre and I would like to see what tricks you can do."

The ogre, who liked to show off his tricks, immediately changed himself into a snarling lion.

"Very clever," said the cat, "but a lion is large, and I think it would be more impressive to change into a tiny mouse."

At once the ogre changed into a little mouse, and the cat pounced on him and ate him up!

Then the cat went into the castle. He told all the servants that their new master was the Marquis of Carabas, and that the king was coming to visit them.

When the king arrived at the castle, the cat purred, "Your Majesty, welcome to the home of the Marquis of Carabas."

The cunning cat told his master to ask the king for his daughter's hand in marriage. And that's what he did!

The king, impressed by the nobleman's wealth, agreed and soon the Marquis of Carabas and the princess were married.

The cat was made a lord of their court and was given the most splendid clothes, which he wore proudly with his fine boots. And they all lived happily ever after.

The Story of the Blue Jackal

Once upon a time, there lived a jackal named Chandarava. One day, he was very hungry. He couldn't find any food in the jungle, so he wandered into a nearby village to search for something to eat.

The dogs in the village saw him and started to chase him. Trying to escape, Chandarava ran into a house. It belonged to a washerwoman. Inside was a big vat of blue dye. Without thinking, Chandarava jumped into the vat to hide. His entire body was dyed blue. When he climbed out, he no longer looked like a jackal.

The dogs were confused. They had never seen a blue animal before. Terrified, they ran away.

Hungry and fed up, Chandarava returned to the jungle. The blue dye wouldn't wash off! When the other animals saw him, they were frightened and ran away. Chandarava didn't want to be alone, so he came up with a clever plan.

"Don't be afraid," said the blue creature. "The Lord of Creations has sent me here to be your king and to protect you. Come and live in peace in my kingdom."

The other animals were convinced by Chandarava's words.

"O, Master, we await your commands. Please let us know whatever you want," they said.

The blue jackal gave everyone jobs – mostly to serve him! He enjoyed being treated like royalty, but he was also a kind and fair ruler, and the animals lived peacefully together.

One evening, after enjoying a particularly fine feast, Chandarava heard a pack of jackals howling in the distance.

Unable to hide his natural instinct, Chandarava howled back. When the other animals heard this, they realised that Chandarava was only a jackal and not the king he was pretending to be.

Chandarava knew he had been wrong to fool the animals. He tried to explain why he had lied, but it was too late. The animals were so angry that they chased him out of the jungle.

So the blue jackal ended up spending the rest of his days alone after all.

The Princess and the Pea

Once upon a time, a king and queen lived in their castle with their only son. They were growing old, and it wouldn't be long before the prince would need to take up the throne. But before he became king, the prince wanted to find a princess to be his wife. He wanted her to be clever and funny and loving and kind.

The prince travelled the world in search of a real princess, but none of the princesses he met was quite right.

Then, one stormy night, there was a loud knock on the castle door.

"Who could be out on such a terrible night?" cried the queen.

The king rose to his feet. "Whoever it is, we must let them in and offer them shelter."

The prince helped his father pull open the castle's heavy doors. To their astonishment, a girl was standing outside, shivering in the rain.

"Good evening," she said politely. "Please may I come in? I was travelling when I lost my way. I'm cold and wet."

"You poor thing," cried the queen. "You must stay here."

The prince could not stop staring at the beautiful girl. "What's your name?" he asked.

"I'm Princess Sophia," she replied.

At the word 'princess', the king looked at the queen. The queen smiled and took the girl's hand.

"Let's get you some dry clothes," she said.

That evening, over supper, the prince chatted with the charming girl. She was everything he had dreamed of, and by the end of the evening he had fallen in love!

The queen was happy for her son, but she wanted to make sure Sophia was a real princess.

She got her maid to help her pile up twenty mattresses on the guest bed. Under the bottom mattress she placed a tiny pea.

Then the queen showed Sophia to her room. "Sleep well, my dear," she said.

The next morning, the queen asked Sophia how she had slept. Sophia looked pale and tired.

"Not too well, I'm afraid," said the girl. "There was a hard lump in the bed and now I'm covered in bruises."

On hearing these words, the queen laughed and hugged Sophia tightly.

"We have found our princess!" she cried. "Only a real princess would be delicate enough to feel a tiny pea through so many mattresses!"

"I knew it!" grinned the king.

The prince dropped down on one knee.

"Sophia, would you do me the honour of marrying me?" he asked.

Princess Sophia's eyes sparkled with happiness.

"Yes," she nodded. "I will!"

The prince married his bride that very day and they all lived happily ever after.

This all happened a long time ago. If you are passing by the castle, be sure to visit its museum. There's a very special exhibit on display, in a dusty glass case – a tiny, shrivelled pea! Proof of a real princess.

153

Pinkabella and the Fairy Goldmother

Pinkabella loved pink almost more than anything else… and she loved LOTS of things, like playing with her friend, Violet, and spending time with her godmother, Auntie Alura.

Pinkabella often thought her auntie might be a fairy godmother. She always looked so sparkly and magical!

One day, while Pinkabella and Violet were playing in Pinkabella's bedroom, Auntie Alura came to visit.

"Auntie," cried Pinkabella, flying into her godmother's arms.

"It's lovely to see you too, Pinkabella," Auntie Alura laughed, hugging her back. "Is this your room? It's very…"

"PINKTASTIC!" beamed Pinkabella.

"PINKERRIFiC!" added Violet.

"Er, yes," said Auntie Alura, casting her eye around Pinkabella's things. "Although I've always preferred gold, myself!"

Pinkabella looked at her auntie's gold dress, gold shoes and gold bag, and grinned. Auntie Alura really did like gold!

"Maybe she's my fairy GOLDmother," Pinkabella whispered to Violet with a giggle.

Just then, Pinkabella's dad called up from the garden. "Pinkabella! Violet! Come and get a drink." And the two friends rushed downstairs, leaving Auntie Alura alone in the bedroom.

A while later, after Auntie Alura had joined them outside, Pinkabella and Violet returned upstairs.

"Eek!" gasped Pinkabella as she opened her bedroom door. "My pinktacular room is all… GOLD!"

"B-but how?" asked Violet, in shock.

Suddenly, Pinkabella saw a sparkly stick on her bed.
"This looks like a wand," she gasped.
"Do you think it's magic?" asked Violet.
Pinkabella grabbed the stick. "Let's try it!"
She waved the wand and said, "Make everything
PINKTASTIC again!"
The wand made a fizzing noise, and pink sparkles shot
out of the end…

The sparkles whizzed through the air, and everything they landed on turned bright pink.

"Wow! It IS real," cried Violet. "Let me have a go!"

Pinkabella threw the wand to Violet, but it bounced off the wall and flew out of the open window.

Pinkabella and Violet watched in horror as the wand twirled away, shooting pink sparkles down into the garden.

Pinkabella and Violet ran outside. Everything had turned pink, including Pinkabella's mum, dad and auntie!

"My wand!" cried Auntie Alura. "What's it doing out here?"

"I found it on my bed," replied Pinkabella. "I'm really sorry, Auntie Alura. I didn't know it was your wand. I just wanted my room to be pink again."

"It's okay. I'm sorry, too," said her auntie. "I wanted to see what your room would look like in gold, but then I forgot to change it to pink again. I must have left my wand behind by mistake."

After Auntie Alura had turned everything back to normal, Pinkabella asked her why she had a wand.

"I'm your fairy godmother, of course," she whispered. Pinkabella gasped in delight. She had been right all along!

Then Auntie Alura added a touch of gold to Pinkabella's dress.

"Pink and gold together," laughed Pinkabella. "It's magical!"

Ella's Year

Ella's daddy always moaned about the weather.

"It's too windy," he grumbled in spring. Ella laughed.

"Wind is fun," she said, helping him to fly a kite high in the air.

In summer, Daddy didn't want to play outside.

"It's too hot," he said. "I need to cool down."

"Sunny days are fun," said Ella. She held Daddy's hand and they ran to the cool, blue sea for a splash and a paddle.

When autumn came, Daddy frowned.

"The fallen leaves are too messy," he complained.

"They're beautiful," said Ella. She showed him how to rustle and crunch through the leaves on the walk to school.

Soon, winter arrived.

"It's too cold," said Daddy. "There's nothing good about winter."

"Winter is the best season of all," said Ella, and she pulled him outside to build a snowman.

Daddy laughed. "I may not always like the weather," he said, "but I love playing with you, Ella!"

Rosie's Surprise

Rosie longed to ride a horse at the stables, just like her brother, Ben. But Ben only let his sister muck out the stalls.

"You don't know anything about horses," he told her. "You can watch me ride while you clean."

Then, one morning, when Ben was trying to ride his newest horse, it refused to budge or do anything it was told.

"I bet I can help," thought Rosie.

So the next day, she got up early and went to see Ben's newest horse. Instead of jumping on its back straightaway, like Ben did, Rosie spent time grooming its coat and talking in a soothing voice. Soon, she and the horse were friends. When Ben arrived, Rosie was trotting around the stable yard on its back.

"Rosie," cried Ben, "you're amazing!"

"So, can I can ride your horse too?" Rosie asked.

Ben laughed. "Yes, and I'll muck out the stalls today. I want to watch you and learn some tips!"

Cinderella

Once upon a time, there was a young girl who lived with her father, stepmother and two stepsisters. The stepmother was unkind, and the stepsisters were mean. They made the girl do all the housework, eat scraps and sleep by the fireplace among the cinders and ashes. Because she was always covered in cinders, they called her 'Cinderella'.

One morning, a special invitation arrived. All the young women in the kingdom were invited to a royal ball – a ball for the prince to choose a bride!

Cinderella longed to go, but her stepsisters just laughed.

"You? Go to a ball? In those rags? How ridiculous!" they cackled.

Instead, Cinderella had to rush around helping her stepsisters get ready for the ball.

As they left for the palace, Cinderella sat beside the fireplace and wept.

"I wish I could go to the ball," she cried.

Suddenly, a sparkle of light filled the dull kitchen, and a fairy appeared!

"Don't be afraid, my dear," she said. "I am your fairy godmother, and you SHALL go to the ball!"

"But how?" said Cinderella.

"Find me a big pumpkin, four white mice and a rat," replied the fairy godmother.

Cinderella found everything as quickly as she could. The fairy godmother waved her wand and the pumpkin changed into a magnificent golden coach, the white mice became white horses and the rat became a coachman.

With one last gentle tap of her wand, the fairy godmother changed Cinderella's dusty dress into a shimmering ball gown. On her feet were two sparkling glass slippers.

"Now, off you go," said the fairy godmother, "but remember, all this will vanish at midnight, so make sure you are home by then."

Cinderella climbed into the coach, and it whisked her away to the palace.

Everyone was enchanted by the lovely stranger, especially the prince, who danced with her all evening. As Cinderella whirled round the room in his arms, she felt so happy that she completely forgot her fairy godmother's warning.

Suddenly, she heard the clock strike midnight...

BONG... BONG... BONG...

Cinderella picked up her skirt and fled from the ballroom. The worried prince ran after her.

BONG... BONG... BONG... She ran down the palace steps, losing a glass slipper on the way, but she didn't dare stop.

BONG... BONG... BONG... Cinderella jumped into the coach, and it drove off before he could stop her.

BONG... BONG... BONG!

On the final stroke of midnight, Cinderella found herself sitting on the road beside a pumpkin, four white mice and a black rat. She was dressed in rags and had only a single glass slipper left from her magical evening.

At the palace, the prince saw something twinkling on the steps – a single glass slipper!

"I will marry the woman whose foot fits this glass slipper," he declared.

The next day, the prince took the glass slipper and visited every house in the kingdom.

At last, the prince came to Cinderella's house. Her stepsisters tried and tried to squeeze their huge feet into the delicate slipper, but no matter what they did, they could not get the slipper to fit. Cinderella watched as she scrubbed the floor.

"May I try, please?" she asked.

"You didn't even go to the ball!" laughed the elder stepsister.

"Everyone may try," said the prince, as he held out the sparkling slipper. And suddenly...

"Oh!" gasped the stepsisters, as Cinderella's dainty foot slipped easily into it.

The prince joyfully took Cinderella in his arms.

"Will you marry me?" he asked.

"I will!" Cinderella said.

Much to the disgust of her stepmother and stepsisters, soon Cinderella and the prince were married.

They lived long, happy lives together, and Cinderella's stepmother and stepsisters had to do their own cleaning and never went to a royal ball again.

Why the Sun and the Moon
Live in the Sky

Long ago, the Sun and the Water were great friends, and they both lived on the Earth together. The Sun visited the Water often, but the Water never returned his visits.

At last the Sun asked his friend why he never visited. The Water replied that the Sun's house was not big enough, and that if he came with all his family, he would drive the Sun out of his home.

"If you want me to visit you," the Water added, "you will have to build a very large house. I have a huge family and we take up a lot of room."

The Sun promised to build a very large house and soon afterwards, he returned home to his wife, the Moon.

The Sun told the Moon what he had promised the Water, and the next day, they began building a large house to entertain the Water and all his family.

After several weeks, the house was complete and the Sun asked the Water to come and visit him.

When the Water arrived, he called out to the Sun and asked whether it would be safe to enter.

"Yes, of course. Come in," replied the Sun.

The Water began to flow in, followed by the fish and all the other animals and creatures that belonged to the Water.

Very soon, the Water was knee-deep in the house.

"Is it still safe for us to come in?" called out the Water.

"Yes, of course," replied the Sun. So more of the Water's family came in.

When the Water was at the level of a man's head, the Water said to the Sun, "Do you want more of my family to come?"

Not knowing any better, the Sun and the Moon both said that everyone was welcome. More and more of the Water's family came in, until the Sun and the Moon had to sit on top of their roof.

Every so often, the Water asked the Sun if it was still okay to come in. Each time, the Sun and the Moon answered yes.

Soon, the Water overflowed the top of the roof, and the Sun and the Moon couldn't see their house any more.

As the Water rose higher and higher, the Sun and the Moon climbed up into the sky… and they've been there ever since!

Pixie Pool

Lilian wasn't enjoying her day at the beach.
"I'll never learn to swim," she said. Even with floats
and armbands, Lilian found swimming tricky. So she went to
explore some rock pools. One of them sparkled like diamonds.
When Lilian peered more closely, she saw a pixie sitting
beside the pool. Lilian gasped in surprise.

"Please don't tell anyone you saw me!" cried the pixie.
"If you keep my secret, I'll grant you a wish. What will it be?"

"Please can you make me swim as gracefully as a dolphin?"
Lilian asked.

The pixie smiled. Just then, Lilian heard dolphin voices
calling to her from the sea. "We'll help you!" they said.

Lilian splashed into the water and the dolphins jumped
and dived around her.

"This is fun!" Lilian said, joining in. Suddenly, she was
gliding through the water, just like the dolphins.

When they left, Lilian waved and carried on splashing.
She couldn't wait for her next beach trip!

Show Time!

Isabelle the rabbit and her friends looked forward to the woodland summer show all year long. But this year, there was a problem.

"The show's cancelled!" cried Hazel the mouse. "This year's act, The Amazing Moles, are all ill in bed."

The other animals felt gloomy – except Isabelle.

"We're not giving up that easily," she said. "We can put on the show."

"How?" asked Magnus the squirrel.

"Practice makes perfect," said Isabelle.

So the friends rehearsed their favourite dance routines, jokes and magic tricks, while the audience gathered. Then the show began with a tap dance by Hazel and her sister Jessica. Magnus told jokes, and Gabriel the owl did magic. Finally, Isabelle performed a ballet dance. The crowd went wild!

"Being in the show was even more fun than watching it," said Isabelle, hugging her friends. "Let's do it again next year!"

Swimming Lessons

Mother Duck was a very busy duck indeed.

"I'm going to visit my poorly friend Mrs Goose and take her some food," she told her five babies. "I want you all to be good and do lots of swimming practice while I'm gone."

"We will," said Charlotte Duck. And all her brothers and sisters nodded and promised. But as soon as Mrs Duck had disappeared from sight, the ducklings jumped, splashed and belly-flopped into the water. They lay on lily pads and spun around until they felt dizzy. They tipped upside down and waggled their legs in the air.

"Those aren't your lessons!" exclaimed a nearby frog. "You should follow the rules."

"Jumping and splashing is much more fun than following the rules!" replied the five little ducks.

"You're going to be in trouble," said the frog, hopping away.

The ducklings looked at each other. Now they felt sad. They hadn't meant to be naughty, and they didn't want to get into trouble, so they sat quietly on the bank of the stream.

Just then, they heard Mummy Duck singing as she swam home. Bravely, they told her what had happened. Mummy Duck listened carefully. Then she smiled.

"Well, even though you didn't follow your swimming lessons properly," said Mummy Duck, wrapping her soft wings around them, "I'm pleased that you told me the truth. Now, let's practise swimming together."

After swimming practice, Mummy Duck told her ducklings that the lesson was over and it was time to play. Then with a big SPLASH, she belly-flopped into the stream!

"After all, you learn best when you're having fun!" she said.

The Snow Queen

Once, there was a wicked imp who made a magic mirror. Everything it reflected looked ugly and mean. One day, the mirror smashed into tiny specks, and the specks got into people's eyes and made everything look bad to them. Some specks became caught in people's hearts, making them feel grumpy.

A few of the specks from the mirror floated towards a far-away place where there lived two best friends, called Gerda and Kay.

The pair spent endless days together. In the winter, Gerda's grandmother told them wonderful stories while the snow swirled outside.

"The Snow Queen brings the winter weather," she would say. "She peeps in at the windows and leaves icy patterns on the glass."

In the summer, the children would play in the little roof garden between their houses.

One sunny day, they were reading together when Kay let out a cry. Specks from the imp's magic mirror had caught in Kay's eye and his heart.

Kay became bad-tempered throughout the summer and the autumn, and was still cross when winter came.

One snowy day, he stormed off with his sledge. Suddenly, a large white sleigh swept past and Kay mischievously hitched his sledge to the back.

The sleigh pulled him far, far away. When it finally stopped, Kay realised the sleigh belonged to the Snow Queen from Gerda's grandmother's story! The Snow Queen kissed Kay's forehead and her icy touch froze his heart. He forgot all about Gerda and his home.

Back home, Gerda missed Kay. She searched everywhere for him. Just as she was about to give up, Gerda noticed a little boat among the rushes down by the river.

"Perhaps the river will carry me to Kay," she thought. She climbed in and the boat glided away.

Many hours later, the boat reached the shore. A large raven came hopping towards Gerda.

"I have seen your friend," the raven croaked. "A young man who sounds like him has married a princess. I'll take you there."

That night, the raven took Gerda to the palace. But the prince wasn't Kay.

Poor Gerda! She was far from home. She told the prince and princess her story. They promised to help her, and the next morning Gerda was given warm clothes and a golden sleigh.

She set off into the woods, but before long she was spotted by a band of robbers.

"That sleigh is pure gold!" they hissed.

The robbers sprang out and captured Gerda. Then the daughter of the robber chief appeared. The girl was lonely and excited by the thought of a new friend.

"Please, treat her gently!" the robber girl pleaded. "She can stay with me."

Gerda was grateful to the robber girl for her kindness.

Inside the robber's den, Gerda met the robber girl's pet reindeer. When Gerda told her new friend about Kay, the reindeer spoke, saying he had seen Kay with the Snow Queen.

"I know the way to the Snow Queen's palace," added the reindeer. "I will take you there."

It was a long, cold journey, but at last Gerda and the reindeer arrived outside the Snow Queen's palace.

Inside the ice palace, the Snow Queen still held Kay under her spell.

"Spring is coming," she announced suddenly. "I must leave. It is time for me to make it snow on the other side of the world!"

And she flew off in her sleigh, leaving Kay alone.

At that moment, Gerda crept into the palace. When she saw her friend, she wept. Her tears fell onto his chest. They melted his cold heart and washed away the speck of glass. Kay began to cry too, and his tears washed the glass from his eye. At last he was free of the spell!

The reindeer carried Gerda and Kay back home.

"Grandmother!" called Gerda. "We're back at last!"

The old lady hugged them tightly. She was so happy to see them.

"I knew that you would come home one day," she cried. "Now, tell me all about your adventures!"

Alfie and Alice

Alfie and Alice were best friends. They went everywhere together. Alfie loved Alice. He thought she was the kindest owner a dog could have. Alice loved Alfie. She thought he was the cutest dog in the whole wide world.

And Alfie and Alice both LOVED their food. Whenever a delicious food smell wafted near Alice's little button nose and Alfie's shiny black nose, the pair of them would dash off to follow the scent.

One day, Alice and Alfie were playing hide-and-seek in the park. Alfie was hiding but Alice couldn't find him anywhere.

Alice called and called, but Alfie didn't come bounding over like he usually did.

"Try not to worry, Alice," said Mum, gently. "I'm sure he can't have gone far."

Alice wiped away her tears and sniffed the air.

Suddenly, she had a great idea.

"Mum," she cried excitedly. "I know how we can find Alfie. We've got to follow the food smells!"

Mum grinned. "Of course! Alfie LOVES his food."

"And I can smell pizza," shouted Alice. "Come on, let's go!" and she rushed off towards the small café by the duck pond.

"Have you seen a little brown dog with black patches?" Alice called out to the café owner.

"Oh, I think he went that way," said the man, and he pointed towards the bandstand.

"This way, Mum," said Alice. "I smell sausages!"

Alice and her mum followed the delicious smell wafting across the grass. When they reached the bandstand, they could see a group of musicians huddled around a smoking barbecue, cooking their lunch.

"Have you seen a little brown –" Alice started to say. But then she saw something…

"Alfie!" Alice cried. There, in the middle of the group, sat Alice's dog. He was eating from a plate of sizzling sausages.

Alice hugged Alfie tightly.

"Don't ever disappear again!" she scolded. "Now, let me have one of those sausages. Yum!"

The Fisherman and His Wife

One day, when the sea was blue and calm, a poor fisherman set off to work. At first, he caught nothing. Then, when the fisherman was about to call it a day, he felt a tug on his line. The fisherman struggled to reel it in.

"This must be a big fish," he thought.

The fish was enormous, and the fisherman was very pleased. But his pleasure turned to surprise when the fish spoke to him.

"Please throw me back," pleaded the fish. "I am not really a fish at all, but an enchanted prince."

The stunned fisherman gently let the fish back into the water and set off for home.

The fisherman and his wife were so poor that they lived in a wooden shed. When he told his wife about the talking fish, she was angry with him.

"You fool!" she cried. "No wonder we're so poor, if you can't see a good thing when it's biting you on the nose!"

The fisherman's wife told him that if the fish was an enchanted prince, he should have asked for something in return for setting him free.

"Go back to the same spot tomorrow and catch that fish again, and this time ask him for a little cottage so we can live a better life," said the fisherman's wife.

The next morning, when the sea was green and choppy, the fisherman set off again. He rowed out to the same spot as the day before, hoping to see the magical fish.

"Enchanted prince, please hear my plea, jump out from the water and talk to me," called the fisherman.

The fish appeared and asked the fisherman why he had called him. The fisherman explained that he was a very poor man and would like to live in a little cottage instead of a wooden shed.

"Go home," said the fish. "Your wish is granted." And he left with a SPLISH!

So the fisherman returned to his wife, who waved to him from the window of their lovely new cottage.

The fisherman's wife was pleased for a little while, but soon became unhappy again.

"We could have asked for more from that magic fish," she told her husband one evening. "This is only a small cottage; a castle would be much better." And she begged her husband to go and find the magical fish, and ask him to grant her wish.

The next morning, when the sea was purple and rough, the fisherman set off again and rowed out to the same spot as before.

"Enchanted prince, please hear my plea, jump out from the water and talk to me," called the fisherman.

The fish appeared, although he didn't seem very happy about being called again. The fisherman explained that his wife found the cottage rather small, and would prefer to live in a castle.

"Go home," said the fish. "Your wish is granted." And he left with a SPLASH!

So the fisherman returned to his wife, who waved to him from the window of a grand castle.

But the fisherman's wife wanted even more. "If that fish can give us a grand castle, he can make me a queen," she said.

The next morning, when the sea was grey and murky, the fisherman set off again and rowed out to the same spot as before.

"Enchanted prince, please hear my plea, jump out from the water and talk to me," called the fisherman.

The fish appeared, not at all pleased to be called again. The fisherman explained that his wife now wanted to be a queen.

"Go home," said the fish. "Your wish is granted." And he left with a SPLOSH!

So the fisherman returned to his wife, now a queen.

"If that fish can make me a queen, then he can make me the ruler of the whole world!" said the fisherman's wife.

The next morning, when the sea was black and stormy, the fisherman rowed out to the same spot as before.

"Enchanted prince, please hear my plea, jump out from the water and talk to me," called the fisherman.

The fish appeared. He was furious. The fisherman explained that his wife now wanted to be the ruler of the world.

"Go home," said the fish. "Your wife has what she deserves." And he left with a SPLISH, SPLASH, SPLOSH!

The fisherman returned to his wife... who was living in the wooden shed again.

Her greed had indeed been rewarded!

Harper's Rainbows

It was the perfect day for rainbows, and Harper wished she could play outside in the rain and sunshine with all her friends. But she was feeling poorly. So her mummy tucked her up in bed with a hot water bottle and a book.

"If only I could see a rainbow," she told her mummy.

Harper's mummy felt sorry for Harper. Then she had an idea. She invited all Harper's friends over and gave them each a tin of paint and a paintbrush. As soon as Harper fell asleep, they tiptoed into her room. Swish! Swoosh! They carefully painted every wall and even the ceiling, filling her room with bright rainbows. When Harper woke up and saw them, a huge smile spread over her face.

"I love rainbows!" she said. "My amazing friends have made me feel better already!"

Jungle Shower

Grace the elephant loved showering under the biggest waterfall in the jungle. She splashed and sang at the top of her voice. But the other animals wanted a peaceful shower time.

"Stop singing!" shouted the monkeys.

"Stop splashing!" squealed the parrots.

"But shower time should be fun," said Grace. She felt sad that the others weren't having a good time. Then she had an idea.

"Everyone loves bubbles," she said. "I'll make shower time so much fun that they have to enjoy it!"

She put her trunk in the water, then lifted it up to the sky… and blew! Bubbles rose and danced on the breeze, popping around the animals. The monkeys, parrots, giraffes and everyone else started to smile. Soon the jungle was filled with bubbles and the sound of Grace's singing – and everyone joined in!

Alice and the White Rabbit

One day, Alice was sitting beside a river with her sister when something curious happened – a white rabbit with pink eyes ran past.

"Oh dear! Oh dear! I shall be too late!" he said. Then he took a watch out of his vest pocket and hurried on.

Alice followed the rabbit down a large rabbit hole. The rabbit hole went straight on like a tunnel for some way and then dipped so suddenly that she found herself falling down…

"I must be getting near the centre of the Earth," Alice thought to herself. Down, down, down Alice kept falling.

Suddenly, she landed in a heap at the bottom. When she got up, she found herself in a long hall, lined with doors. At the end was a little three-legged glass table. There was nothing on it but a tiny golden key. Alice tried the key in all the doors, but it wouldn't open any of them. Then she noticed a low curtain she had not seen before. Behind it was a tiny door.

She turned the key in the lock and it opened. The door led into a beautiful garden, but Alice could not even get her head through the doorway.

She went back to the table and saw a little bottle labelled "DRINK ME!"

Alice drank it and shrank. But she remembered that she had left the key on the table. Alice didn't know what to do. Then, she saw a cake marked "EAT ME!"

Alice ate it and began to grow. Soon, she was so large that her head touched the ceiling!

Alice began to cry. She was wondering what to do when who should come along but the white rabbit? He was carrying a pair of white gloves and a large fan.

"If you please, sir…" began Alice.

The rabbit dropped the gloves and fan, and scurried away.

"How strange everything is today," said Alice, picking up the gloves and the fan. "I'm not myself at all." Then she began fanning herself as she wondered who she might be instead.

After a while, Alice looked down at her hands. She was surprised to see that she had put on one of the rabbit's little white gloves.

"I must be growing smaller again," she thought.

Alice realised that it was the fan that was making her shrink, so she dropped it quickly and ran to the door. Suddenly, she remembered that the key was still on the table.

"Drat," she said. "Things can't possibly get any worse." But she was wrong. SPLASH! She fell into a sea of her tears.

"I wish I hadn't cried so much!" wailed Alice.

Just then, she heard something splashing. It was a mouse.

"Do you know the way out of this pool?" asked Alice.

The mouse didn't reply.

"Perhaps he speaks French," thought Alice. So she began again. "Où est mon chat?" which was the first sentence in her French book and meant "Where is my cat?"

The mouse leaped out of the water in fright.

"I'm sorry!" cried Alice. "I didn't mean to scare you."

"Come ashore," said the mouse. "I'll tell you why cats frighten me."

By this time, the pool was crowded with birds and animals. There was a duck, a dodo, a parrot, an eaglet and other curious creatures too. Together, they all swam to the shore.

The birds and animals were dripping wet.

"Let's have a race," said the dodo. "It will help us to dry off." And he began to mark out a course.

Then everyone began, starting and stopping whenever they felt like it. It was impossible to tell when the race was over, but after half an hour they were all very dry.

"But who won the race?" asked the mouse.

"Everyone," said the dodo. "Alice will give out prizes." So Alice handed around some sweets she had in her pocket.

"But she must have a prize, too," said the mouse.

"What else do you have in your pocket?" asked the dodo.

Alice handed over a thimble and he gave it back to her, saying, "I beg you to accept this thimble."

Alice accepted as solemnly as she could and then they all sat down to hear the mouse's tale. But Alice was so tired, she just couldn't concentrate, and she drifted off to sleep.

The next moment, she woke to the sound of her sister's voice. "Wake up, Alice!" said her sister. "What a long sleep you've had!"

"I've had such a curious dream!" said Alice, who told her sister all about it. And what a wonderful dream it had been!

The Fox and the Crow

One day, a crow was flying past an open window when she spotted a tasty piece of cheese on the table. There was no one in the room, so she fluttered in and stole it! Then she flew up into the branches of a nearby tree, and was just about to eat the cheese when a fox appeared.

The fox was also particularly fond of cheese and he was determined to steal the crow's prize.

"Good morning, Mistress Crow," he greeted her. "May I say that you are looking especially beautiful today? Your feathers are so glossy and your eyes are as bright as sparkling jewels!"

The fox hoped that the crow would reply and drop the cheese, but she didn't even thank him for his compliments. So he tried again: "You have such a graceful neck and your claws are really magnificent. They look like the claws of an eagle."

Still the crow ignored him.

The fox could smell the delicious cheese and it was making his mouth water. He had to find a way to make the crow drop it.

At last he came up with a plan.

"All in all, you are a most beautiful bird," he said. "In fact, if your voice matched your beauty, I would call you the Queen of Birds. Why don't you sing a song for me?"

Now, the crow liked the idea of being addressed as the Queen of Birds by all the other creatures in the woods. She thought that the fox would be very impressed by her loud voice, so she lifted her head and started to caw.

Of course, as soon as she opened her beak, the piece of cheese fell down, down, down to the ground. The fox grabbed it in a flash and gobbled it up.

"Thank you," he said. "That was all I wanted. I have to say that you may have a loud voice, but you don't have a very good brain!"

And the moral of the story is:
Be wary of a flatterer.

Balloon Adventure

Freddie had always wondered what it would be like to fly like a bird. One evening, he talked to his dad about it.

"Oh, it would be amazing!" said Dad. "Looking down on the world, soaring through the clouds... I know, why don't we organise a balloon ride, then we can see for ourselves!"

"That would be awesome, Dad!" cried Freddie, excitedly. "We'll be able to see everything from a bird's-eye view."

So a few days later, on a warm, breezy evening, Freddie and his dad set off on their balloon adventure.

They settled into the big wicker basket, and then they were off... floating higher and higher. Up, up and away in the big pink balloon!

Freddie couldn't believe his eyes...

Up above, he could see planes soaring through the clouds.

"I wonder where they are going?" he sighed, as he watched their fluffy vapour trails fade into the distant sun-tinted skies.

"Look over there, Freddie," cried Dad, pointing at a flock of birds.

They soared past, flying in a V formation.

As the breeze rustled through his hair, Freddie glanced down. Everything looked tiny! Houses and trees appeared in miniature, like models. The cars crawled along winding ribbons of roads like marching ants.

Dad grinned at Freddie. "How are you enjoying your ride?" he asked.

"It's so cool," laughed Freddie. "I feel like I'm a bird, too. I can't believe we are so high in the air!"

The balloon drifted along silently and over the crest of a hill. Suddenly, the sky was filled with other balloons of all shapes and sizes. Freddie could see a smiling elephant and an inflated bear with a sleepy face. Hovering nearby was a shimmering butterfly and a funny bunny balloon.

"A balloon carnival!" cried Dad, smiling and waving as they floated along on the breeze with the other balloons.

Freddie glanced off into the distance. He could see the silhouette of a city, and the sun was beginning to dip towards the horizon. It was time to head home.

Slowly, the balloon glided lower and lower, down and down… until it landed with a gentle bump on the ground.

Freddie hugged his dad.

"Thanks, Dad," he said. "This has been the best day EVER!"

Dad smiled. "Let's go on another balloon adventure soon."

The Butterfly Ballerina

Isabella Ballerina loved ballet. Best of all, she liked going to Madame Colette's Ballet School.

"Let us practise our ballet positions!" called Madame Colette one morning, clapping her hands. "No, no, Isabella! You are pointing the wrong foot again!"

"Sorry!" Isabella said. "I'm always getting my left and right mixed up!"

"Now, girls," cried Madame Colette. "I have exciting news to announce! We will be putting on our first show, the Butterfly Ballet. I will choose girls to play raindrop butterflies and rainbow butterflies, and one girl to dance as the sunshine butterfly!"

Back home, Isabella told Mum all about the ballet show.

"I just wish I could remember my left from my right!" she sighed.

Mum smiled. "This might help." She gave Isabella a beautiful butterfly bracelet. "Wear it on your right wrist. Then you'll always be able to tell which way is right."

At each ballet lesson, Isabella kept looking at her butterfly bracelet to make sure she turned the right way!

Finally, after many rehearsals, Madame Colette told the girls their roles.

"Isabella, you shall play the sunshine butterfly. As you twirl so beautifully, you will dance the final pirouette!" said Madame Colette.

Isabella smiled. She just hoped she would turn the right way!

The week before the show, Isabella practised her pirouettes everywhere! She twirled in the garden… in her bedroom… and at the park.

On the night of the big show, all the girls dressed in tutus and shimmering butterfly wings. The lights dimmed. Beautiful music filled the room. The ballet was about to begin!

The raindrop and rainbow butterflies danced gracefully from flower to flower.

At last it was Isabella's turn to dance. Nervously, she touched her butterfly bracelet. Then, taking a deep breath, she twirled the most perfect pirouette she had ever twirled!

The girls joined Isabella on stage, and they all curtsied.

"Oops!" giggled Isabella. She had curtsied with the wrong foot forward, but it didn't matter one little bit.

She would always be Isabella, Butterfly Ballerina!

The Princess and the Salt

Once, a rich and powerful king summoned his three daughters to his throne room on his birthday. His first daughter gave him gold and the second daughter brought him silver. The king was very pleased with these gifts.

"I have brought you salt," said the third daughter.

"Salt!" cried the king. "How dare you insult me? What good is salt?" And he banished his own daughter from his kingdom.

But when the princess left, all the salt in the kingdom vanished. At first, the king complained that his food was tasteless, but then he became very ill from lack of salt.

The king realised how foolish he had been and sent for his daughter. When she returned to the kingdom, the salt also returned.

"Forgive me," said the king. "Your gift of salt was more precious than silver or gold, for you cannot live without salt."

From that day on, the king learned to value things other than his riches.